CW00377292

GOOD

GIRL

GONE

BAD

EMMY ELLIS

DI KANE BARNETT ALSO FEATURES IN
ALL THAT DECEIT
A DI TRACY COLLIER NOVEL

PROLOGUE

She's a good girl is Charlotte. Or she was until recently. She's changed, more's the pity, and I'm not sure if I want to do anything about it. I think for now I'll let her be. You know, get on with things, live life.

Life. That's a funny thing, isn't it? Here one minute, gone the next.

Especially if I have anything to do with it.

See, look at her there, that old woman, my neighbour, who's annoyed me for ages. She has a habit of setting things on fire in her garden, no matter the weather. Tonight, there's a bloody gale going on, yet there she is, *burning things*.

The bonfire is a big one—too big for a residential area. Sparks fly in all directions, orange and hot and tongue-like, ready to scorch if they had a mind.

I wish they'd scorch the silly bitch tending to it.

She's prodding the base where she's stacked up wood and all sorts—blimey, might even be a chest of drawers down there if I'm seeing it right. The amount of flames dancing about are enough to boil a body alive.

Now there's a thought.

Would she smell like the old lady she is if she caught alight? Would her flesh sizzle? Would her hair give off that aroma, same as when you singe your moustache with a match while sparking up a fag?

I expect so. Yeah, I expect so.

And I'm about to find out.

ONE

She'd fucked him, plain and simple. Hadn't expected him to ask for a repeat performance, though, now or at any other time in the future. Christ, she'd got herself into a bit of a mess, hadn't she?

How the hell do I get out of this?

"Look," she said, while he ogled her from the rumpled bed, "you agreed to a one-night stand. I told you in the pub I couldn't do more than that. You said you understood." She felt a right wally standing there in just her knickers, so she shoved her legs into her navy-blue jeans.

He rammed his fingers through his hair as though he verged on pulling it out. "What I understand is, your boyfriend is a prick."

Tell me something I don't know.

"Yes, well, that's neither here nor there, is it? I told you about him so you'd get the gist of why this can't be anything more." She fancied pulling her own hair out. Couldn't lose her composure, though. She had to leave without her fuck buddy creating a scene. If any of the staff here saw her, if he decided to go off on one, they might remember her, and who knew how many people Jez was friends with?

Jez was the aforementioned prick. Good name, that. Suited him.

This bloke here had snuck her in the back exit of the hotel earlier, and she hadn't seen a soul. Might not be the same on the way out.

God…

"Just agree to meet me again, see how it goes. Can't do any harm, can it?" He smiled—rakish-looking sod.

"It could do *a lot* of harm. If Jez finds out…" Her heart beat too damn fast for her liking. She was out of her depth. Stupid of her to have done this, to come out tonight while Jez was busy doing God knew what, her ending up here having had the best shag of her life and unsure how to handle the fallout.

"Who's going to tell him?" he asked. "I'm not. Fuck that."

His last two words set bells off in her head. Did he know Jez more than he'd let on earlier when she'd whinged about him? Granted, there weren't any other men around here with that name, so it stood out among the Michaels and Peters, but...

Bollocks.

"Don't tell me you know him," she said, doing up her jeans then reaching for her sparkly black jumper.

"Might do." He smirked. "Might also know your name's Charlotte. Charlotte Rothers with the long black hair she likes having wrapped around my fist."

She paused with her top halfway over her face. It struck her that she didn't even know *his* name.

What was I thinking?

Her pulse pounded in her ears, and she yanked her sweater on, cursing — she'd forgotten to put her bra on first. It dangled off a dingy light-blue lampshade on the cabinet next to the bed, empty hills of cerise fabric that mocked her.

You've been a bad girl, Charlotte.

Oh God, I'm so in the shit.

If she lost it now, she'd never get home before Jez. She'd have to hole up somewhere — couldn't be her mum's place, she wasn't allowed there, or with Felicity, either, her mate from years back who she hadn't seen since...too long ago — but then if she *did* leave Jez, where would she be? Still on Jez's radar, that's where, a bloody bright flashing light letting him know she'd had enough of their relationship and was up to no good.

"Listen, what about giving me some time to think?" She should buy a few days, get some space, work out what to do between now and whenever she contacted this fella again.

"I know where you live, Rothers."

Somehow, that didn't sound sinister coming from him. He was a right sexy bugger. Problem was, he seemed to know it. So why was he interested in *her*? Jez had told her recently she was washed out — 'A shell of your former self,' he'd said, and she'd thought: *Looked at yourself recently, have you?* He'd swanned out, hadn't he, all bluster and bullshit, and she'd gone to the mirror to have an honest-to-goodness gander at herself to see if he was right. Of course he was. Her hair had been faded, lifeless, and she'd stopped wearing makeup ages ago. What was the point anyway, when Jez didn't seem bothered with her? All he was concerned about was going to the pub or meeting elsewhere with his mates, while she sat at home bored off her tits.

So she'd dyed her hair—freshened it up, that had—and bought some new foundation, the kind that didn't sit in your wrinkles like clogged sand.

"Then it's better that you stay away," she said. "If you know Jez, you know it isn't the best thing to do, coming to our place." She stepped over to the bed to collect her bra then stuffed it into her bag. She hoped Jez wouldn't be back when she returned. If he found out she'd left the house, if he looked inside her bag... "I can probably get out again tomorrow night. He's off drinking in some new club or other, so he said."

Probably picking up some new tart and all.

"What about seven o'clock at The Orange Pebble?" he asked, scratching his dark stubble.

The sound did funny things to her.

"It's out of the way." He sat up, the sheet falling to concertina at his waist. "Jez never goes there."

"How do *you* know?" She slipped her red high-heeled shoes on then tottered over to the mirror to sort her hair.

"Because he's a person of interest," he said.

Jesus fuck. Only the police spoke like that. "You what?" She would have spun from the mirror to face him, but he grinned at her in the reflection. "It isn't funny. Are you a damn copper?"

He swung his legs out of bed, sat on the edge, dangling his hands between them. His hair stuck up every which way, reminding her of a kid who'd tossed and turned during a nightmare.

Was he *her* new nightmare? One to add to all the others? Waking nightmares, she had. Every damn day saw her crossing a minefield, hoping the bombs didn't go off. And him, that man right there, was a massive bomb.

He sighed. "All right, I'm a copper, but don't let that bother you. I'm the same as any other bloke, just got a job that puts the shits up people, that's all. Besides—" His phone rang, and he answered it without saying hello.

Rude git.

Someone on the other end spoke for what seemed an age, and Charlotte reckoned she should leg it now while he was occupied. She crept over to the door, glancing back to check he wasn't watching, but he was in front of her in an instant, one hand raised, finger pointing.

He shook his head at her and said to whoever was on the line, "Um, right. I'll be there in a minute." He ended the call, gripped her arm, and led her back to the bed. "Sit there for a second, all right? I need to be somewhere, and it just happens to be your street."

God, what's Jez gone and done now?

8

"My street?" *Parrot much?* "Erm, why?"

"Death in your road, apparently." He shrugged into his shirt. "Shouldn't be telling you that, but you'd have heard soon enough anyway."

"Who?" she asked, hoping it was Jez. All her problems would be gone then.

"Neighbour of yours."

Her heart sank.

Bloody wicked, you are, wishing your old man had karked it.

He pulled on his suit trousers—black, faint pinstripe—then sat to roll on his socks—burgundy, a moss-green diamond pattern up the sides—and finally his jacket. He sliced his fingers through his hair, dipped his head to look in the mirror, then swiped up his phone and keys. "Come on, let's be having you."

He laughed at that, but Charlotte didn't find it remotely funny. Anything copper-related set her teeth on edge—cost a fortune they had, those screw-in types that gave you a brilliant-white smile. Jez had escorted her to the dentist. She wasn't allowed out much on her own.

"I shouldn't turn up with you," she said. "What if Jez sees me?" Her stomach somersaulted, and she told herself off for being such a whiny prat.

"He won't. I'll drop you at the end of the road, then you can walk home." He moved to the door, resting his fingers on the handle. "Bear in mind, though, there'll probably be a cordon up, and you'll have to prove who you are to get past it. Got any ID on you?"

She envisaged inside her purse—all she had in it was a ramp-up-the-interest-charges credit card and her bank debit card—the secret one Jez didn't know about, and she hid it deep down in the slot behind her National Insurance card so he wouldn't see it. "Nothing that will prove I live there, no."

"Well, it's a good job I'll be the one letting you through then, isn't it?" He opened the door and stepped out into the corridor. "All clear."

She followed him down the hallway, and wasn't it just fucking peachy that the thud of the door shutting had her thinking it was ominous, like she was locked out of the safety of that room—her life—forced to move ahead into the unknown?

If Jez ever got a whiff of what she'd done, *she'd* be dead.

Her feet hurt. What had possessed her to wear these toe-pinchers she'd never know. She usually put slippers on, what with being at home virtually twenty-four seven, there for whenever Jez wanted a meal—meals he didn't bother eating half the time. He'd told her, when they'd first got together, he didn't want any queen of his working.

Queen, my arse. Treats me more like a maid.

As she trailed the copper out of the building and into the car park towards his metallic-grey Fiat, she admitted why she'd gone out tonight. She'd fancied a bit of love — sex was love, wasn't it? — and someone to care about her for a while. She'd got that, all right, and now he wanted more.

So did she.

I can't get away from Jez. He'll find me. Said I belong to him and no one else.

And the perverse side of her had wanted to go out, maybe to get caught. Perhaps this was the kick up the arse she needed. She'd seen another side of love with this bloke here, and it had been nothing like it was with Jez. Not that they shagged much these days. Last time they'd done it had been months ago.

Got a new queen, have you, you dirty fucker?

"Get in," the copper said, unlocking the doors with a press of his key fob.

She did, buckling up and sinking down so only her eyes and the top of her head would be visible through the windows.

He sat in the driver's seat and started the engine.

The journey didn't take long — minutes — but it might as well have been hours. Paranoid someone would spot her, Charlotte steadied her nerves, then exited the car at the end of her

11

street. She sensed the copper's gaze on her, so she bent to look in at him.

"Give me two minutes, then I'll be at the cordon," he said.

She nodded, legs going weak, and wedged herself partway inside a hedge outside number three, her stupid jumper getting caught on grasping branches. He drove off, and she asked herself if she wanted to be with a man like him—one on the right side of the law instead of the wrong. She couldn't risk it. Jez was a nasty bastard. He'd kill a copper, no problem.

She studied the street. People were out on the kerb, nosing at the comings and goings. What she wouldn't give to not live here. It had been sixteen years—sixteen God-awful years, if she were honest—except if she left, she'd miss Henry Cobbings at number fourteen. He'd saved her sanity more times than she could remember. She enjoyed listening to his stories, his voice, even if he bordered on being a bit boring sometimes.

Her house had stood in darkness when she'd left. Now it was blacked out save for the living room light blaring. Why Jez didn't just switch on a lamp... Reckoned he liked the outrageously expensive bronze chandelier hanging from the ceiling, with its eighteen candle bulbs that gave off enough brightness to blind you.

Shit, he's back early.

Anxiety kicked in. Where could she tell him she'd been? Why hadn't she concocted a cover story beforehand? He'd know she'd been out on the piss by smelling her breath. And her get-up wasn't her usual outfit these days. Normally, unless she was visiting Henry or the shops, she camped out on the sofa in lounge pants and an old T-shirt. Last time she'd gone out with Felicity, so long ago now it was almost forgotten, Jez hadn't just smelt her breath. He'd checked between her legs, saying it was his right to sniff out some other dirty bloke who'd shagged his bit of stuff.

She hadn't been with anyone that night—but tonight?

What if he smells me again?

She wrenched her attention away from her house to where the copper had parked. He stood by the cordon, and she waved—*stupid, stupid cow!*—then dropped her hand to her side, praying Jez wasn't looking out of the window and had seen what she'd done.

She walked up the street, head held high, as if she had nothing to hide and hadn't been doing the dirty tonight. She reached the copper.

"ID please," he said.

She showed him her credit card, and he nodded, lifting the cordon.

"Don't forget to act surprised when you get in," he said, winking.

13

She ducked under. "Right. Yes. Um…Officer…what?" She'd get his bloody name out of him if it was the last thing she did. "You know, just in case another policeman asks me who let me through."

He smiled—that rakish one again—and her knees jolted like they had when she'd first met Jez. That wasn't good. Dangerous, all of this…this…whatever the hell it was.

"DI Kane Barnett." He shook her hand.

You shouldn't have done that. Now I remember what it was like when we—

He let her hand go. "At least you have an alibi for tonight, eh?"

Christ, she hadn't thought about that side of things. Her stomach plummeted. "What? I can't tell anyone I was with *you*. You sound about as sharp as a marble suggesting that."

"Don't worry." He sniffed. "Say you were at the pub. I'll vouch for you. Say you saw me there and recognised me again just now, all right?"

"Okay, if you think that'll work." She smiled a bit tightly, lips closed, but she was hardly in the mood to give him a gimpy, teeth-baring grin, was she.

"We'll make it work." He swallowed. "Seven tomorrow. The Orange Pebble."

She nodded. "If I can get out. It depends…" She bit her lip. "Well, he's home already, and I—"

"Here's my card." He handed it to her.

She took it, white with some form of gloss on it, the words embossed, bobbly beneath her thumb.

"If you need me—for giving me information about the investigation, for Jez purposes—then call." He messed about with his hair again—a habit?—then shoved his hands into his trouser pockets.

Charlotte walked away, her legs heavy, as though they didn't want to take her home. Funny how your body knew the best thing to do before your brain and heart.

At her gate, she looked back, but Kane Barnett wasn't there. Maybe he'd gone into the house of the dead person. She didn't know who it was. Still, Jez would be sure to tell her. He loved giving her information, almost as though he gloated that she'd never know anything because she was virtually caged up at home.

Bastard.

Bastard he might be, but she had to gather the courage to lie about her evening.

But he'd spot the lies, no doubt about it.

He always did.

TWO

Charlotte slid her key in the lock, but the door swung open on silent hinges—Jez had a thing about using WD40. He'd squirted it in her mouth once when she'd given him some lip; he hadn't had any soap close by at the time.

She squealed, whipping her hand up to her mouth, heart thundering.

Jez stood there, face like a slapped arse she'd bet, but she couldn't see it clearly to know for sure. He filled the doorway, arms akimbo, fists clenched. The vibrant light from the living room to the right cast a slice of not-quite-white brilliance, creating an aura around his body, showing his shaved head dotted with the pinprick beginnings of new blond hair growth. His actual features were murky, though, his nose, mouth, and hipster beard draped in shadows that hid his spiteful expression—and there was no way it wouldn't be spiteful.

"Get in, you bloody slapper."

He stepped aside, and she almost—almost—turned away to seek safety with Kane, but she'd been conditioned, hadn't she, to do as she was told. She hated herself for crossing the threshold, for allowing herself to be in a situation that was crap at best and wicked at worst, but cross it she did.

His knee jabbing into her backside sent her skittering forward, her damn shoes squeezing her toes and abrading her heels. She didn't cry out in shock—she'd expected as much from him—and instead headed for the living room, where she could hopefully take her shoes off before he got hold of her and—

"Not in there," he said.

She toed her shoes off, dropped her bag beside them, then turned to face him. God, she detested the way she trembled, how she'd allowed one man—all right, one bloody scary, bully of a man—to send her back to childhood where she felt ten years old, insecure and frightened.

"Up there." He jerked his head towards the stairs.

So it was going to be *that* sort of punishment, was it?

Resigned to her fate, to being found out for her deception within the next few minutes, she trudged up the stairs. Why hadn't he asked her where she'd been? Why hadn't he slapped her so hard her head smacked against the wall like he usually did? She never visited Henry Cobbings after that sort of reprimand. He'd want to hurt Jez if he saw the evidence of a beating, and she couldn't have that. It was bad enough she'd blurted out to him one time that Jez hit her.

'Why do you stay with a bloke like that, Char? There's a man out there for you who wouldn't do that sort of thing, you know that, don't you?'

The soft carpet taunted her on her way up. If only she matched her home—well-cared for, something to be proud of, even though the expensive furnishings had been purchased with ill-gotten gains. Drug money, she reckoned, going by the battery-operated scales and the baggies she'd found under the sink the other

18

month. Jez sniffed a lot lately, too, and she wouldn't be surprised if he was ramming coke up his nose.

At their bedroom door, she hesitated, dreading going in, because when she did, there was no going back. Not that she had a choice with Jez barrelling up the stairs now, his big, beefy body heavy, the landing floor creaking in protest.

Shame he didn't spray WD40 on *that*.

"Not in that one, you silly cow, the back room." He disappeared in there, sniffing loudly then sneezing.

She sagged against the jamb with relief, although the darkness surrounding her seemed oppressive and threatening. She could go downstairs now, run out of the front door in her bare feet, the peppering of tarmac nuggets on the pavement digging into her soles. She'd find Kane, tell him she needed help, protection, anything, something. He'd offer her the chance at staying in a safe house like they did on TV, but who was she kidding? Jez had told her once that if she thought she'd get help from the police, she had another think coming. They didn't dish safe houses out to just anyone, he'd said. No, she'd have to hide herself somewhere, and one day, he'd come knocking, just you wait and see.

She shuddered, steeling herself to join him in the back bedroom. He had a gym of sorts in there, and she hoped he didn't tie her to the sit-up bench like he had before and kick the living daylights out of her.

"What are you hanging about for?" he groused. The strike of a match meant he was sparking up a fag. "Shit or get off the damn pot. You're missing the good bit."

She frowned, yet again asking herself why he wasn't questioning her about leaving the house. Mind you, he'd done this before, lulled her into a false sense of security, letting her think everything was hunky-bloody-dory, when it wasn't.

It really wasn't.

She didn't answer him — past experience had taught her not to, and what with her alcohol breath... She sidled into the room, squinting in the gloom. He stood at the window and had parted the curtains a foot or so, the peach glow of the streetlight in the road to the rear of their garden peeping through the branches of a huge chestnut tree. It did her nut in come autumn, that tree, shedding its leaves all over the grass, giving her more work to do. Jez didn't like leaves on the grass. He'd bought that fake stuff, and it reminded her of a butcher's shop window — like anyone would really lay meat out on the bloody grass—and she hated it. Always slipped arse over tit when it was wet.

"Look," Jez said.

She moved to stand beside him, her lungs tight, and she needed a wee. Fear did that, didn't it? Sent you to the loo more often than not.

"They're going to put a tent up in a minute, so get your fill," he said.

Charlotte peeked out to where Jez pointed. A bright light, halogen if she was any judge, lit up the garden a few doors down, one like they had at football stadiums. Wasn't it odd to light it up like that before the tent was in place? They didn't do anything of the sort on the programmes she'd watched. All the neighbours this side of the street would be gawping like she and Jez were, seeing things they shouldn't see, taking pictures and uploading it to social media, the whole world able to see what she assumed was the last resting place of Mrs Smithson. It had to be the old lady, didn't it? Otherwise, why were there loads of coppers milling about down there?

She properly took in the scene. The remnants of a bonfire sat wet and soggy in the centre of the old woman's lawn—if the scrubby grass mixed with mud patches could be described as such.

"You can just make out the shape of the old baggage on top if you look hard enough," Jez said, grinning, his teeth slightly amber from the streetlight.

I want to bash those teeth in.

And what he'd said wasn't fair. Mrs Smithson wasn't an old baggage, she was kind and helpful, always there with a cup of sugar if you needed it, although her keep having bonfires had become a bit of a pest recently, especially when Charlotte had hung the washing out on the line.

Jez didn't like smoky-smelling laundry.

Mrs Smithson usually set her fires during the day, though, which wasn't on really, so why had she started one tonight?

Charlotte imagined the woman had been burning secrets—letters from long ago, maybe written by a lover, or someone she'd confided in, and the author had mentioned the old lady's misdemeanours, and she had to get rid of the evidence.

Thinking stuff like that got her through most days.

"That'll sort the fires then. Won't need to go round there anymore and give her what for," Jez said, wheezing out a smoker's laugh.

It sent a shudder through her.

Please, God, help me to get away from him.

Still she didn't respond. She couldn't work out whether he was playing a game or genuinely wasn't bothered she'd been out. That wouldn't be true to form, though, so what was he planning next? She'd given up trying to read him, to gauge his behaviour. He changed his MO so often, she couldn't make head nor tail of it.

"Anyway," he said. "Where's the milk?"

Milk?

Her repeating that in her head reminded her of her time with Kane, where she'd mimicked his words. Why hadn't she stayed in that hotel room, asked him to get her away? To another town, perhaps, where she could change her name by deed poll, hiding out in bliss, although she'd always be looking over her shoulder.

"Are you having a thick-as-pig-shit moment, Char?"

She swallowed. Nodded.

"You went to the shop to get some milk and, like a good girl, you tarted yourself up to go — you know I don't like people seeing you in your drab crap. Lounge pants, guaranteed to turn your bloke off. Why don't you wear that launjeray stuff anymore?"

"I...the *lingerie* doesn't look nice anymore. It's sixteen years old. Um, I...I didn't get the milk because..." *Go with it. If he's testing you, it doesn't matter. You'll be walloped either way.* "I heard

23

people talking in the shop, about someone being killed in our road, and I rushed back in case—"

"In case it was me? Dunno why you'd think that. I was out when you went, you dozy mare." He stared out at the goings-on again, his nose twitching.

"How did you know I went to the shop?" She spoke softly so her booze breath didn't waft in his face.

"Cobbings told me. If I didn't know better, I'd say he fancied you."

"He's old, Jez, and just a friend." *What the hell is wrong with him?*

"Yeah, well, make sure it stays that way and all. Bet he's a dirty pervert behind closed doors. You might want to watch yourself next time you go. He could feel you up with those wrinkly hands of his. Imagine that."

Jez had even managed to taint the one happy thing she had in her life—her visits to the older man, where she pretended she was someone else for the hour or so she sat beside him on his brown corduroy sofa with powder-pink velour cushions, tassels on each corner, the strands knotted from years of use.

"Right, I'm off out. Only nipped back to get something. Forgot to take it earlier, didn't I. Could have knocked me down with a feather when I saw the street lit up like Christmas with the police car lights. Bloody hate that colour blue."

Crap yourself, did you, thinking they'd come for you?

I wish they bloody had.

"Anyway," he said. "Don't do anything I wouldn't do. Oh, and next time, no milk or not, don't go to the shops late again. There are nasty people about after nine o'clock."

There's nasty people out in daylight. Like you.

Nine o'clock, he'd said. So he'd come home around then, had he? It hadn't been much later when she'd arrived, so the timeline fitted. Yes, she could have got to the shop and back in those twenty-odd minutes. She stopped herself from blowing out a long breath of relief. If he would just leave now, she could get into the bathroom to wash Kane off her and brush her teeth, then Jez wouldn't be any the wiser.

Unless he wanted sex. Then he'd know.

Why didn't I insist on a condom with Kane?

"So," Jez said, "I'll get the milk from the late-night garage on my way back. Can't be doing without it in my coffee of a morning."

He headed out, filling the doorway for a moment, and the sight suffocated her, her imagining he blocked not only that exit, but her exit out of this life.

She didn't ask where he was going, who he'd be meeting, and it slapped her then, the palm of realisation hard and spiteful, that she didn't give a shit what he was up to. Why had it all gone so wrong? Why had he changed so quickly once she'd moved in? What had she done to turn him off her, turn him into the pig of a man he now was?

She didn't have any answers. If she did, maybe she'd have fixed this long ago.

Waiting until the front door clicked shut, she went into their bedroom and, despite disliking herself for falling into old patterns, she peeked out through a gap in the slatted blinds to watch which direction he took.

He crossed the street then stood beside a few other neighbours, arms folded over his chest. What, was he getting off on this or something?

She shuddered at how she didn't know him at all. How could he want to stand there like that? Didn't he have some tart waiting for him in a pub? And what had he come back home for? He'd said he'd forgotten something. Whatever it was, it was easily slipped into a pocket, because he didn't hold a bag or anything.

Disgusted by him, she turned away, rushed downstairs to switch off the living room light, then walked into the bathroom and set the shower to hot. Once under the spray, she removed the head from the holder and sluiced herself down below, hoping it would remove any evidence should Jez paw her once he got home. And she'd let him, would go through the motions, all the while tears spilling onto her pristine white pillowcase that smelt of yellow Lenor, her thinking of England, Spain, and every other country on the planet just to get herself through the ordeal.

And she'd continue this way until she could be free.

THREE

She'd struggled, that Mrs Smithson. I should have known she would. All flailing arms and legs—even kicked me in the shin, she did. That pissed me off quite a bit. Who knew someone so old would have such strength?

It's cold out. I'm standing watching like all the others, but I really should be getting on.

Thing is, I don't want to. It's great being here, out in the street, knowing those policemen are scurrying about in the old baggage's garden over something I've done. Ants, so many ants, that's what those PC Plods are.

Debbie from along the way comes over, smiling at me with her brace-covered teeth, her fifteen-year-old body a joy to the eyes. If I were younger, or she were older, I'd pop her cherry whether she wanted me to or not. But I can't be doing with being caught out like that—don't fancy that being on my résumé, so to speak, so she's safe. For now. Who knows what'll happen once she hits sixteen, eh?

"Hiya!" she says in that way she has, chirpy and bright.

She reminds me of Charlotte all those years ago, when we first met.

Time flickering by is such a bitch.

"You can't turn back the clock," so my sister used to say, "you just have to march on."

My sister had rung the cancer bell, but six months later that bastard disease had come back. She hadn't rung the bell again. If I hear them, like when I walk past the school during playtime and the teacher rings one, it brings on grief so heavy, so all-consuming, I'm fit for nothing. I told Charlotte all about it, back in the early days. She'd cried and suggested I buy a bell and ring it from time to time, to get used to it, to disassociate myself with what the sound represents.

I tried. It didn't work. Having the bell sitting on the mantelpiece is just about all I can cope with.

How have sixteen years swept by so quickly, though? How has Charlotte gone from a vibrant eighteen-year-old to what she's become? Shocking, it is, not to be bothered about yourself anymore. Still, there's a reason for it, and I'll get her to admit to it eventually.

In the meantime, I'll march on for my sister.

"All right?" I ask Debbie. "How are you diddling?"

She laughs, throwing her head back, and her curly auburn hair sways, the ends peeking out from either side of her in turn, a pendulum, tick, tock, tick, tock. "You *are* funny." Her smile vanishes as quickly as it had arrived, her expression sober now, as though she's just remembered why we're out here. "Terrible, isn't it? You know, about what's happened to Mrs Smithson?"

"Terrible, yes." I could laugh, because it isn't terrible. The old bat needed getting rid of. She was a nuisance with her bloody fires. "Sometimes life isn't fair, is it?"

Like how I can't run my hands all over your skin.

"No," Debbie says then sticks her bottom lip out. "And she was so nice, too," Debbie goes on, "although Mum and Dad were a bit narked about her bonfires. Someone over there said they reckoned her death was *because* of the bonfires. Isn't that a bit wack?"

Not by any means.

"Yes," I say. "Silly to think that."

"That's what I thought." She lifts a strand of hair to her mouth, drapes it across that gorgeous bottom lip, and sucks on it.

Revolting habit. It's put me off her, and maybe she needs reprimanding for that kind of behaviour. Women need to be put in their place, don't they, and she could do with being taught the lessons sooner rather than later.

"Shame," she says. "I used to like going round to her house. She made me Belgian buns with more than one cherry on top."

"Oh, you could come to see me, if you want." *Yes, the lessons, you could learn them then.* "If your mum and dad wouldn't mind, that is."

"Why would they?" She frowns, and it's unbecoming, spoils her pretty face. "It's not like they don't know you, is it."

"Oh, I dunno. People say things, don't they? Untrue things about other people. They could say I was a kiddie fiddler having a teenager in my house."

"I'm sure it's all right to go round yours, but I won't say anything if it makes you feel better.

When can I come? Tomorrow, after school maybe?"

I think of the daylight, and that would just mess everything up. "Oh no, I'm busy then. What about at eight o'clock? Will that do you?"

"Great! I'll get my homework done before that. Can you bake Belgian buns?"

"No, but I can get some from the bakery for you. And some Coke." I laugh.

Coke...

"Okay," she says. "Well, I'm off then. Shouldn't really be out here—got some maths I ought to be doing. See ya."

She saunters off, hair tick-tocking again, and the beast in my underwear perks up, but not at her body this time, or the thought of smoothing my palms over her skin.

No, I'm thinking about the lessons.

FOUR

Kane stared at the remains of Mrs Smithson, the covering of the marquee thankfully shielding her from view now. Good job they'd got it up in time. It had pissed down straight after; could have wrecked the scene.

This poor old dear — why the hell had she done this to herself? He hadn't a clue so far. All the neighbours the uniforms had spoken to said she was a nice lady who'd do anything for anyone, so her death was strange. Why throw yourself on a fire? What was all that about?

He sighed, blowing the air out through chicken's arsehole lips. He felt for the woman, he really did, but her death couldn't have come at a more inconvenient time. He'd been with Charlotte Rothers for a reason — to get info on Jez so he could be put behind bars once and for all. The thing was, Jez, being a slimy bastard, had kept his true business away from his girlfriend. That's what Kane had surmised anyway. Seemed she didn't have a clue what her bloke got up to once the sun went down.

In the pub, she'd spoken about Jez's day job — mechanic, so she reckoned, but that was all a load of bollocks. Jez was no more a mechanic than Kane was a criminal. Yeah, the man might go home with a bit of oil beneath his fingernails, but he'd have put it there on purpose. Jez ran a drug shop, Kane was sure of it, but he couldn't just stroll into Jez's fake garage and demand to search the premises.

The bloke was cute — and not in the sweet way. He knew how to keep his head down, how to disappear even though he was being followed by Kane or some other copper. At times, Jez was there, then he was gone, like someone had spirited him away.

It drove Kane up the wall.

He hadn't meant to go to bed with Charlotte, but she'd been so damn pitiful when telling him about her life with Jez that he'd just wanted to give her some attention. He didn't usually sleep with people off the cuff like that, or while on the job, so his actions had surprised him. She'd wanted a one-night stand, and that had been fine with him, until she'd cried halfway through and told him she'd never had sex like it. Never been held the way he'd held her.

Shit.

He didn't need this complication, and he felt a right bastard for asking to see her again. That had been his intention all along — you know, gain her confidence, make her see there were places out there she could go to get away from her bully of a boyfriend. He wanted to help her do that, too, but he'd shagged her, hadn't he, and things could get messy now. She'd find out he'd been using her, and he'd look a wanker.

Despite that, he'd continue with his plan, only he wouldn't take her to bed again. He'd get back on track, get her sorted somewhere safe, then hopefully nail that son of a bitch for a long stretch.

He sighed again and shook his head. This case here, in the form of fire-ravaged remains, would have to take priority, and that pissed him off. He was *this close* to ensuring Jez Pickins went down, and if he took his eye off the ball, he'd lose the damn game.

Jez one, Kane nil.

Not going to happen.

"Boss?"

He turned, his white overalls scrunching, and faced DS Richard Lemon, an older fella sporting floppy ginger-grey hair and an orange monster of a moustache. His ruddy cheeks spoke of him loving whisky, his nose bulbous and red from overconsumption. His liver was probably pickled, but Kane couldn't see the man giving up the booze now. If he had to guess, he'd say Richard took shots in his coffee throughout the day. He smelt of it constantly, and it usually churned Kane's stomach.

"All right, Richard? Nice to finally see you," Kane said. "Where the bloody hell have you been?"

"Sorry. Got caught up in something. Didn't have my phone on."

Kane narrowed his eyes. "Not good form, Richard."

"I know. Like I said, sorry." Richard coughed.

The air from it smacked Kane in the face. "You…uh…you been on the sauce?"

Richard reddened even more. "I was off duty."

"So was I, but I managed to only drink one pint. You never know when we'll be called out."

"We have to have a life," Richard grumbled, rocking back and forth, his white-bootied feet rustling on the sodden mud beside the bonfire.

Thank fuck the photos have already been taken. He could have buggered this scene right up the way he's digging his heels into the ground. He needs to retire.

"So what do we have here then?" Richard asked.

The change of subject wasn't lost on Kane, but he let it go. Couldn't be arsed with explaining how being a copper wasn't a nine-to-five job. He was tired, riled, and needed sleep. "A Mrs Smithson decided to chuck herself on her bonfire—no apparent reason so far. Neighbours said she's nice, wouldn't hurt a fly, the usual gumph." Christ, he sounded sour.

"Interesting." Richard looked like he didn't give a shit.

Probably wants to get home to Johnnie Walker.

"Not much we can do here now, really," Kane said. "Just got to speak to Gilbert. Maybe he'll give us something to go on after he's seen the body—or what's left of it. House-to-house has already been done. We'll go through the statements tomorrow."

Richard's mouth flopped open. Johnnie's scent crept out of it again. "What, you mean you're going home in a minute? Bloody hell, I needn't have bothered coming. Thanks a bunch." His top lip curled, lifting up his moustache hairs.

Kane got up in Richard's face, clenching his hands into fists. "Listen, I didn't fucking call you, all right, so don't take this out on me. The chief rang me, and I got here within eight minutes of the call. I was having a damn good evening, as it happens, and it got derailed. I was actually working overtime, unlike some people around here."

He stalked off towards the house. Something had to be done about Richard. The man was past it, not much good these days—not on the job anyway.

As Kane reached the back door leading into a dining room cluttered with too much seventies furniture, knick-knacks on every available surface, and a tiger-striped shaggy carpet that belonged on a tip, not in a house, he stopped. Gilbert stood beside the scarred wooden table, staring out into the garden, his mouth agape.

"Shut it, Gilbert, you're catching flies." Kane grinned.

"Hey, Kane. Rum business this, isn't it." Gilbert came outside and stood on the pathetic excuse for a patio—six slabs, unevenly laid, bulging moss mounds growing out of the four-inch-wide gaps between flags, a dandelion hunched over as if in sadness. "Killed herself, did she?"

"So it seems." Kane shrugged. "I doubt you'll be able to give me anything tonight, will you? She's charred, but it doesn't look like she's burnt all the way through. I don't think she was on there long enough."

"Maybe she took an overdose beforehand or slit her wrists. Nowt strange as folk. Come on, let's have a butcher's." Gilbert ambled off, disappearing inside the marquee, his white forensic suit blending with the rear inside of the tent.

Kane followed, wanting out of his own suit and into a pair of lounge pants. This day needed to fuck off and do one. He'd had enough.

Beside the bonfire in the tent, Kane stood while Gilbert examined the remains. After he'd done his usual checks, Gilbert turned the body over. The hunks of burnt wood beneath her slithered against each other, as wet as the ground under and around them. Neighbours had put out the fire, having come in through Mrs Smithson's front door, seeing as it had been wide open.

Had she wanted someone to save her and they'd been too late?

"Ah," Gilbert said.

Kane knew what that meant. The M.E. had found something. "What's up?"

Gilbert pointed to the back of the corpse's head, brushing some of the damp clumps of ash and debris onto a white plastic sheet he'd placed under her. "She's had a knock to the head."

What? "Fuck me, I wasn't expecting *that*."

"Blunt force trauma, I'm afraid. I'd say she was murdered. Too much mess on her noggin to have bashed it herself, on the table corner, say. Besides, the wound shape indicates a pole or something of that description. Long, slim. Think of the iron bar in Cluedo." He chuckled.

"I have no idea how you can laugh," Kane said.

Gilbert glanced up at him and smiled. "You have to in my job."

"I suppose." Although Kane didn't get it. He didn't find this sort of thing funny. Laughing would be disrespectful. Wrong. "Right, well, I'm going home." He eyed everyone in the tent. Richard obviously hadn't followed Kane in and had gone home already. Kane gritted his teeth. If his partner made it into work on time in the morning, it'd be a miracle.

Useless bastard.

Kane left the house, taking off his white suit, the booties, the gloves, and wouldn't you know it, his attention was pulled to the Pickins' house. Typical, when he should be keeping it professional. He wondered whether he ought to go over there, but Jez stood on the path opposite, gazing across at him.

Does he know? Did he beat it out of Charlotte?

40

Kane clenched his jaw and returned the glare. Jez, as bold as ever, didn't break eye contact and lifted a hand. He created a gun shape with his fingers then pointed the business end to his temple. Kane smiled—he wasn't going to let this wanker bother him—and Jez frowned. The bloke was so used to people being frightened of him, it was clear he didn't understand Kane's reaction.

Good. Let him wonder what I'm thinking. Let him be on edge.

Jez rolled his shoulders, flipped Kane the middle finger, then swaggered down the street as though he had a broomstick crammed up his arse. Kane waited until the man was out of sight then strode to his car. He'd be a fool to think Jez's gesture meant he was going to top himself. No, it had been aimed at Kane—*watch yourself, copper, I'm after you.*

Whatever.

Kane sat in his car and eased along the road to stop outside the Pickins'. He scoped out the façade—no light on. Pretentious-as-fuck stone ornaments either side of the entrance, lions as far as he could make out. Fancy knocker, standing out in the light from the street lamp. Slightly mottled glass panels, two of them, filled the top of the black UPVC door. Ah, light shone now, as though someone had opened the door of a room at the top of the stairs.

He waited, battling with himself on whether he should knock and see if Charlotte was okay. Jez was long gone, but if he knew what had happened between Kane and Charlotte, he might come back.

Sod it. I have backup a few feet away. I'll knock her up.

He grimaced at that turn of phrase and hauled himself out of the car and to the front door. The lions stared straight ahead, as if making out they hadn't seen him, wouldn't tell Jez he'd been here. He shook his head to clear out the ridiculous thought and rapped with the knocker.

What he thought were two lower legs appeared at the top of the stairs, a silhouette against the creamy-yellow light backdrop. He sighed, thinking if she *had* taken a slap or two, she wouldn't want to open the door anyway. But the legs moved, blending with the darkness halfway down the stairs until they disappeared, and he straightened his jacket lapels, his stomach doing a number on him. Churning, it was, like he was meeting up with a date.

Sort yourself out, mate.

He blew out a breath. She came towards the door, close, so close she could only be peering through the fish-eye peephole. He'd bet his face looked convex, his nose too big, his eyes recessed. Then the door opened, and she glanced up and down the street.

"Hello. DI Kane Barnett." He held up his warrant card for effect. "I need to ask a few questions." He widened his eyes, willing her to play along.

"Best if you come in," she said and moved back, then to the side a tad.

He walked in. Bloody hell, Jez was making a packet, it seemed. Even just going by the hallway, with the plush white carpet on the stairs and the real-wood floor buffed to a reflective shine, the telephone table that was antique if he wasn't mistaken… Yeah, Jez was raking it in all right.

All those lives he's helping to ruin. I'll have him, mark my words.

FIVE

Charlotte closed the door, mind spinning, legs wobbly. What was Kane *doing* here? Was it to solidify her alibi, prove he'd visited her house to get information on her whereabouts this evening, only to discover she was the bird in the pub he'd seen earlier?

Yes, that must be it.

She led him into the living room, flicking on a lamp via the electronic wall panel beside the door — no common or garden light switches here, everything was state-of-the-art this and up-to-date that.

All pointless. None of it matters.

A soft glow bathed the room, and it was as though she looked at it for the first time, through Kane's eyes. It was posh, no doubt about it, and not something a woman like her should be living in. She didn't come from this part of town, where everyone had money, flash cars, amazing jobs, and more cash in the bank than they could count. No, she was council estate through and through — damn proud of it, too. She'd grown up where the neighbours had been in and out of each other's houses, teabags here, a bit of milk there, maybe even the loan of a tenner if you were short. And street parties whenever it was someone's birthday — God, she'd loved them.

Here, she'd only had the pleasure of talking to Mrs Smithson if the old girl was out in her front garden watching life go by while propping herself up on her black iron curlicue gate. Odd that she had a fantastic front garden but a shitty one out the back — keeping up appearances? And there was Henry Cobbings, her coffee buddy once or twice a week if she could manage it. Everyone else minded their own business, except tonight they were either out in force or nosing through their windows.

Weird how death brought people out of their shells in some respects.

She gestured to the white leather corner sofa, and Kane took a seat on the curve. Charlotte eased herself into the matching recliner — it was Jez's, and she shuddered knowing his arse had touched it, sometimes bare and all — but she didn't trust herself to sit beside Kane.

What if he started talking about what they'd done? For all she knew, Jez could have installed cameras throughout the house — and it wouldn't surprise her. Otherwise, how did he know so many of the things she did while she was alone all day?

She stood abruptly, jerked her head at the door, and said, "I need some air. This has been such a shock. Would you mind if we chatted in the garden?" She copied his wide eyes from when he'd stood on her doorstep, and he nodded imperceptibly then followed her out into the hallway and through the massive kitchen. Self-conscious in her marl-grey lounge pants and baggy Take That T-shirt, she unlocked the back door and stepped outside. Moving over to the patio set — some outdoor wicker jobbie Jez had turned up with, saying he'd got it off the back of a lorry, wink, wink; *ugh, fuck off with those winks, will you?* — she sat in the farthest seat from the house. The branches of next-door's pear tree gate-crashed over the fence, curving above her, a wooden, skeletal hand. A drop of rain from the earlier downfall plopped on her head, cold, and she shivered, patting the bubble to disperse it.

Kane closed the back door then joined her, lowering himself beside her. "What was that all about?" he asked quietly.

"I just...he could have cameras, sound equipment," she whispered, her skin cooling rapidly from the chill in the air. She'd forgotten to cover the patio furniture with the waterproof gazebo last time she'd been out here, and damp from the cream-coloured cushion seeped through to her backside. "The seat's wet. Your suit."

"Doesn't matter." He raised his eyebrows. "I'm only here to establish the alibi and to make sure you're all right. Are you?"

"Yes. Thank you." She shook, remembering what had happened once she'd got home, then it all came tumbling out in a mad rush. She told Kane everything—her need to get away, the lot. "I can't stand it anymore, walking on eggshells. It's doing my head in."

"That's why I approached you in the pub tonight, funny enough. I wanted to help you get away—in return for you helping me *put* him away. Then things...escalated. I didn't mean for it to happen, but I can't say I regret it because I don't."

"How the hell can you help me? I'm rarely able to get out of the house without him finding out about it, and tonight was too much for me. Coming back and finding him here, wondering whether he was going to batter me or not… No one should have to live like that. And I still don't know whether he's hiding something, whether he made it all up about Henry telling him I went out for milk. There was milk in the fridge when I left earlier—I know because I had a cup of tea and had to open a fresh carton. So he's messing with me. Probably tipped the milk away."

She shot out of her seat, her lounge pants sticking damply to her bum, the backs of her thighs, and ran indoors. She swung the fridge door open, the heaviness of it pulling on her arm muscles. It was a double-wide one, same as Americans used, and too big for just the two of them, but Jez had insisted.

The carton of milk sat where it always did, wedged between his Smirnoff and a large jar of gherkins, which he crunched during the rare evenings he was home, right in her earhole.

She wanted to kill him when he did that.

So what did this mean, this milk business? That he hadn't seen it and believed Henry? Or he *had* seen it and was fucking with her mind? She leant more towards the fucking option—and the images that created, of him on top of her, his breath, his hands...

Don't. Don't think about that.

She swallowed bile, slammed the fridge shut, and rubbed her French-manicured acrylic nail over her bottom lip—nails applied by a woman who had a mobile beauty van. Charlotte's lips were slightly sore from kissing Kane. His sharp stubble had made its mark. She lunged towards the odds and sods drawer, rooting around for lip balm. Finding a little pink pot, she rubbed the cream over the faint chaps—raspberry coulis, apparently, though it tasted more like those nasty dried berries mixed with nuts Jez was always forcing her to eat so she didn't put on weight.

She worried some more. Should she leave the milk there? If he hadn't seen it, he'd think she'd gone out again tonight when he'd ordered her not to. But if he *hadn't* seen it, when he went to put a new carton there in the morning, he'd spot the current one.

Her whole body ran cold, and it seemed like she had no stomach, no innards whatsoever. She was just skin, loose and frighteningly without substance, her soul floating inside, desperate to find peace.

She slipped the balm pot into her lounge pants pocket and managed to stagger out into the garden, the door arcing shut behind her.

Once again, the air assaulted her, a stiff breeze coming from nowhere and shunting her towards the patio from behind. Her hair, damp from the shower, slapped forward and whipped against her cheeks, the strands hard, the ends sharp as knife points. One stabbed into her eye, and she cried out, raising her hand to rub it. God, she wanted to scream. To rage at the unfairness of it all, that even her hair, the wind, everything hated her and wanted her to suffer. She made it to her seat and plunked down, her tailbone jarring at the force. Eye watering from not only her hair attack, the other one joining in the pity party, she looked at Kane.

Let him see me in all my manky glory.

She was done — absolutely done — and it no longer mattered what anyone thought of her, not even him.

"What's happened?" he asked.

"The milk. It's…it's still there."

"Shit. Pack some things. You're coming with me." Kane rose and held out a hand.

She took it, drawn to her feet, her body thankfully filling with everything that had seemed missing before. "What about Jez?"

He's going to find me. Kill me.

He stared at her. "I came here to interview you, and you found a letter, didn't you."

"What?" She blinked, her stabbed eye stinging.

"And the letter, it was intimidating, right? Said you'd be next." He squeezed her hand. "Didn't. It."

Realisation gently crept inside her head, and she nodded. "So, what now?"

"You need to be kept safe. You can leave Jez a note, tell him you've been taken to a secure place until the murderer is caught." He winced. "Oh fuck."

"Murderer? What bloody murderer?" Her body threatened to do what it had before and leave her limp, and she fought against it, taking deep breaths, concentrating on the fact that Kane still held her hand, his skin warm, fingers curled, thumb circling.

"I've put my foot in it, so... Mrs Smithson. She didn't kill herself."

What? *What?* "Oh God. No. No, no, no." She slumped back down onto the seat, Kane's hand slipping away, and memories of what Jez had said about Mrs Smithson and her bonfires streaked through her mind—memories of his face every time he'd said he'd clobber her if she lit another bonny. Was it him? Jez? Had he *killed* her?

Charlotte wouldn't have a clue, she hadn't bloody been here, had she. Of all the nights she had to go out, selfishly doing something for herself for once instead of being here where she'd know if Jez had gone round the back and done something to that old lady… Charlotte *always* watched him through the window whenever he left the house, so she'd have *seen* where he'd gone. The whole time she'd been drinking with Kane and moaning about Jez, shagging Kane then worrying about being caught when she got home—and all along Mrs Smithson was being offed.

"It's okay," Kane said. "We'll work this out."

"It was him," she said, her voice quiet. "I think Jez did it."

Kane widened his eyes and again took her hand, pulling her standing. "You don't know that—unless there's something you haven't told me?"

"No, no, I just…it *had* to be him, didn't it?"

SIX

I stub out my ciggie in an alley that looks out onto Jude Street, the tall buildings either side of me a women's clothes shop — used to be Woolworths until the business went to shit — the other selling expensive shoes. Clarks. There are a few *ladies* across the street — using the term loosely there, and loose is right; it's like throwing a sausage up the high street shagging any of them. They're dressed for their job—stockings, short skirts, tits spilling out of too-tight bras. Some even strut about in those bloody nasty tracksuits, the velvet kind, pale pink or purple, can't tell in this light. Whatever they're wearing, they're out on the prowl for punters, and their coven will be one short by the end of the night.

I slip my hood over my head, enough so the front hangs low over my eyes. Can't be having anyone seeing me enough to identify me, can we?

Then I'm walking over the road, heading for the one who looks just like young Debbie. Same hair, same slender build, although this one's a few years older. Still, I can always pretend she hasn't got crows' feet when I'm doing her, can't I. That's what shutting your eyes is for. You can pretend, then, that you're fucking someone else. A bit like the old joke about not looking at the mantelpiece when you're poking the fire.

Handy that.

Debbie Version Two glances over, and she's on me like bird shit on a windscreen, as if I'm something sweet she wants to lick, except there's nothing sweet about me, not tonight. I'm dogged off about Mrs Smithson and Charlotte — don't get me started about her — plus the real Debbie sucking at her hair and ruining everything.

"What are you after?" the prosser asks.

I don't like it when they speak first. "I'm not *after* anything, not from you."

I brush past her, heading for one of the more dolled-up birds. She's a druggy. See enough of them, and you can tell. Seems like she's been on blow or something already, and maybe she needs it to get through the night. Perhaps she even chases the dragon, too, so she can forget why she's here.

I'll make her permanently forget.

I nod at her, and she tries to walk — I say tries, because she's lurching a bit there — and eventually comes to a stop in front of me, her blue eyes bordering on the lightest grey, a dilated black dot in each centre.

Dilated. Yeah, she's on something.

I don't need to say anything else, not to this one. She's made my acquaintance before, which is good for me now. She trusts me.

Bonus.

I was nice to her last time, wasn't I. Gave her an extra wedge of dope as a tip. Money and extras talk and all that. Good job I've got plenty of it then, isn't it?

I lead the way through the alley, the pinging sounds from her high heels telling me she's not far behind. At the end are a few warehouses, some in use, some abandoned, and I head towards an empty one, where windows have been removed, leaving rectangular black spaces. The building's brown bricks, mossed up from years of being in the elements, the pointing dark instead of the pale grey when they'd first been laid, is crumbling. It's a crying shame when a big place like this gets left to its own devices, to rot, when it could be used for something worthwhile.

It's handy for me, though.

I step inside, shoes scuffing over the grit and various oddments where a carpet has obviously been pulled up. A bit of foam backing bumbles off, a tumbleweed, farther into the depths until I can't see it anymore because it's too dark.

Up some stairs, no risers, mind you don't slip through the gaps, then we're on the next level, her skittering along beside me, a chastened dog, albeit without a tail between her legs. Maybe she's remembering what we did last time. She didn't like it but did it anyway.

I much prefer it when women do as they're told.

Unlike Charlotte, supposedly going out for milk, when I know damn well she didn't, not dressed up like that. Not with that amount of makeup on, for fuck's sake, and her hair brushed all nicely, although it made a change to see her looking good for once, like she used to all those years ago.

There's a room just here, which, unlike the others, has a door and no windows, perhaps formerly an office. Whatever it was, it suits my purposes. Her squeals won't float outside through any rectangular, dark spaces, and she can't get away when I shift that big hunk of cement and prop it against the door, though why that's in here I'll never know.

She goes and stands by the wall opposite and waits while I secure the door. I did it last time, too, so she won't think anything of it. I'd let her out on that occasion, so there's no reason for her to think I won't do the same tonight.

I move a few steps towards her and decide what I'll take home with me after. Perhaps that strange little bracelet she's got on. Seems to me it has blue plastic dolphins hanging off it. It's childish, and I don't like it, and every time I look at it, I'll remember her with hate.

Hate enlivens me, gets the blood pumping, and not just through my veins either.

"On your knees," I say.

She complies immediately — *that's what I like to see* — probably thinking she'll get another wedge as well as her payment, and I wonder whether she's smoked all that weed I gave her since then. She didn't ask for anything harder, and if she had, I wouldn't have indulged her no matter how good she is at sucking.

Beggars can't be choosers.

She's doing her thing now, what she's paid to do, and instead of concentrating on what she's at, I'm off in my head, thinking about the things I've yet to do, the women I've got to teach. My dad once told me you can never trust a woman, that they'll wrench your heart out at some point and drag it behind them as they're walking out of your life, taking your home and everything you've earned with them.

Glad I never married. Don't intend to either.

I think of Debbie, and Charlotte, and I'm floating away, content in the knowledge I'll be sorting them soon. I'm drawn out of bliss by another kind, and my world tilts, her down there giving it all she's got. She's choking — *get a grip on yourself, will you, love?* — but I hold her head in place and do the business before she has a chance to get away.

Then I shove her off, and she falls backwards onto her skinny arse, hands flat on the floor beside her, lips plump.

Dirty little cow.

She isn't the woman I want staring back at me like that.

The rage descends then, the mist that clouds everything rational. Illogicality takes its place, and I'm down there on the floor with her, punching her face until blood spurts from her nose. She claws at me, nails gouging my cheek, my wrist, the soft inner side, and I lean down to bite her earlobe and fucking well rip it off.

Swallow.

She screams, as I knew she would, and I press my hand over her mouth and nose. She kicks and writhes, legs and arms all over the place, waving, stalks of corn in the wind, rustling against the floor. And her eyes, they bulge, and she raises her back, me kneeling beside her, clamping my second hand over my other. Pressing, pressing, pressing her head into the floor, knowing it will hurt the little lump sticking out at the base of her skull.

This goes on for a while, too long if I'm honest, then she stills, body mid-arch, fingers like those graspers in the grabby machines at arcades when you can try to win a cuddly toy. She goes limp, back thudding on the floor, but I hold my hands in place for some time after, studying her eyes, not a smidgen of life left in them, the whites marred with red veins resembling cracked windowpanes.

And that's poignant, that is, because eyes are, after all, windows to the soul.

No soul to see here, though.

Before I leave, I pull out my handy tool.

Snip off the ends of the fingers and thumb she scratched me with.

Any of my DNA under those nails is coming with me.

SEVEN

Debbie couldn't wait until the following evening. She had a thing about him for some reason. Mum and Dad would be gutted — they'd say he was too old for her — but she didn't see it that way. She'd heard older men knew what they were doing in the sack, and if the fumbles with the lads at school were anything to go by, she needed someone who'd been around the block a bit. Someone to give her lessons, show her how it ought to be done.

The thing was, if she managed to get him to go out with her, you know, be her boyfriend, they'd have to keep it under wraps, what with her age and everything. But she'd be sixteen soon, not long to wait now, and she could do whatever the hell she liked. It didn't matter that every time she'd spoken to him in the past he'd talked about Charlotte — well, not tonight he hadn't, but there was always a first time for everything, wasn't there.

She'd had a serious think and had decided to definitely keep it quiet where she was going when she visited his place. Say she was off to her mate's house or something, perhaps mention she was hanging out at the park where she usually went. The group of kids she met with normally sat beneath the slide on the benches, where it kind of had a log roof to keep them dry if it pissed down.

Yeah, that would do. And she'd be back at ten like always.

She got up off her bed, her iPod earbud lead snagging on her sociology revision book. At the window, she gazed out. Not many left on the path now it was getting late, just a few stragglers, but he wasn't anywhere in sight. Then he appeared as if she'd conjured him, walking up the street and going towards his house on the opposite side of the road. He stopped to talk to a neighbour still out on the pavement. He went out most nights — she'd been keeping tabs on him since she was thirteen — and she longed to find out where he went and what he did. If it was to the pub, he might take her with him one day. She looked older with makeup on, and if she styled her hair just right, that would add a few years.

She smiled, excitement building in her belly. She couldn't believe he'd actually agreed to her visiting him, and he was buying her some Belgian buns, and Coke, too. What if Charlotte was there, though? And if she wasn't and he talked about her, she didn't know what she'd do or say. Then again, it might be the opening she needed, to find out what was going on between them, see if she could step in and take her place in his affections.

EIGHT

The chat with Kane in the garden had taken a chunk of time, and Charlotte was conscious Jez might be back soon. It was coming up to last orders in the pubs, and although more often than not he stayed for a lock-in, seeing as he'd broken his usual routine and had already nipped back home tonight, she didn't want to take any chances. She'd risked so much already this evening.

She shoved clothes into a black wheelie suitcase, uncaring whether they crinkled from being squashed in there. Best she get away fast than worry about something an iron could fix later.

Tossing in her washbag, containing her toothbrush, toiletries, favourite perfume, hairbrush, makeup, and straightening iron, she was good to go. She zipped up the bag then quickly slung on jeans, a long-sleeved red top, and her comfy boots, sans heels — she couldn't be doing with those again tonight.

Leaving her Take That T-shirt and lounge pants on the floor to piss Jez off one last time, she wheeled the case out onto the landing, recalling the note she'd written to him prior to packing. He'd hit the bloody roof when he read it, but she wouldn't be there to witness it, so thank God for small mercies.

Kane stood at the bottom of the stairs, and he turned to race up and collect the luggage for her. She followed him down, the suitcase bumping on each step, and gave the lower floor a once-over, then met him at the front door.

"Let's go," she said, eager to leave now, to start a new life with Jez behind bars, unable to get to her. As a final touch, she placed the ring he'd bought her – *'No, it's not an engagement ring, you silly cow, it's just a ring. Wear it on a different finger, else people will start talking.'* — on the hallway table. It looked lost on the surface with only the landline phone in its cradle for company.

She switched the outside light on via another electric panel so they could see where they were going and wouldn't trip on any of those stupid decorative stone balls Jez had dotted beside the garden path.

Kane opened the door, and Charlotte was about to tell him to make it quick getting to the car, but *he* stood there, Jez, his face pale beneath his hood, his sleeves pushed up to his elbows as though he'd been in a fight. He lifted one hand to point a finger at her, his eye contact scoring into her soul, her knees jolting so she almost sank to the floor. His wrist had scratch marks, probably where some woman had clung on for dear life while he'd shoved into her, and her stomach roiled, bile burning up her windpipe.

"Where the fuck do you think *you're* going?" he said, eyeing the case at Kane's feet. "And with a copper and all. I thought better of you, Char, fraternising with a pig like this."

He was calm, considering. Probably because a DI stood beside her, the pair of them wedged together, bookends without any books in between. Her heart thundered, and she wished she were anywhere but here, dealing with this, with him.

"I…I left you a—"

"She has to come with me, Pickins," Kane said. "She's had a bit of a nasty shock tonight."

"What, the old dear dying? You were all right earlier, weren't you, Char?" Jez glared at her, his usual tactic of willing her to say yes, to agree with everything he said.

Not anymore. Not now she'd gone this far. Not now Kane was helping her.

"No, it wasn't just Mrs Smithson," she said, "I…I…"

"She received a letter." Kane clutched the suitcase's extended handle, the skin on his fingers stretching white.

"A letter? What sort of letter?" Jez frowned. "Don't fucking tell me you've racked that card of yours up again, and they're sending the bloody bailiffs round. What did you buy this time, eh? *More* clothes you don't even wear?"

She opened her mouth to answer, but Kane knocked her foot with his.

"Not that sort of letter," Kane said. "She's had a threatening one, implying she's next—that she's going to be killed. So, if you'll excuse us, I need to get her to a safe house."

Jez snatched his hood off. Dried blood speckled his temple, a hair's-breadth away from the sideburns that joined his beard. Had that been there earlier? If it had, she wouldn't have seen it anyway, would she, because the house had been in darkness apart from the living room. What had he been up to? She'd thought a couple of minutes ago he'd been in a fight, and perhaps she'd been right. When was he going to grow up?

"As you can understand," Kane went on, "we have to keep her safe. She can come home once things settle down."

She hitched in a breath at that, telling herself he didn't mean it, coming back home, that she'd start life somewhere else, maybe Scotland, or even Ireland would be better. Jez would never find her there with a new name.

Jez didn't take any notice of Kane, staring at her instead. A breeze lifted a fleck of blood, carrying it up to dance beneath the outside Victorian lantern light then dropping it on one of the lion's heads. It settled in a groove carved into its stone mane. "Show me the letter."

"I'm afraid we can't," Kane said. "It's been taken in as evidence by one of the officers already out here tonight." He inclined his head towards the street.

Thank God he'd stepped in, thinking quickly. If it had been left to her, she'd have ballsed it up, mumbling some sort of nonsense, the whole plan ruined.

"So as I said, we need to get going." Kane barged past Jez, clearly unfazed by him, and waited for her on the path.

Jez had staggered to the side, onto the flagstones — he hadn't wanted grass out the front — so Charlotte took her chance and joined Kane, not looking at Jez as she scooted past and followed her saviour, walking between the lines made in the gravel path from the suitcase wheels, out onto the street.

"You'd better be back," Jez called after her.

She didn't answer. Didn't turn around.

She was done with him, done with everything to do with him.

And she was never coming back.

She couldn't get in the car fast enough. She stumbled, her foot catching on something she couldn't see, and she blushed, even though Kane couldn't see her. He was putting her case in the boot, and it whacked shut, him venting his anger, she reckoned. Seat belt on, she waited, then, when he didn't get in after a couple of minutes, she craned her neck to see where he was, and he appeared at the driver's-side window, his tie flapping in the wind. Then was in, beside her, and he clicked the locks, and she immediately felt safer. They pulled away, and she peeked out of the corner of her eye. Jez stood on the step outside the door, between the two lions, three ferocious beasts in a row. A cigarette dangled from his mouth, the orange glow on the end a speck from this distance.

She didn't have to see him again if she didn't want to.

And she didn't.

Hopefully this was it, and she was free.

Kane pulled away from the kerb, and they travelled for a while in silence.

With the evidence of humanity all around her, showing signs of people living their lives — folks walking, heads bent, dogs trotting at their heels; lights going on in bedroom windows, the inhabitants getting ready to turn in; the occasional car slewing past through inch-deep puddles left from earlier — she wondered whether she'd have any semblance of a normal life now. She could turn the clock back, pretend none of this had ever happened, that she'd never met Jez, and if anyone asked, she'd always been single, living alone, no gossip to give them.

Wouldn't that be nice?

Kane swerved into a driveway in front of a house on the only other decent estate in town. His headlights lit up a white garage door with vertical lines a few centimetres apart. Some dirt had stuck in the grooves — *that blood in the lion's mane* — and the silver handle in the centre was at a tilt, as though whoever had been here last hadn't twisted it properly to engage the lock. Perhaps they'd had to be moved and had been in a hurry to get away, the person they'd been running from finding them.

She shuddered, and Kane turned to her. She didn't want to meet his gaze, wasn't ready for that yet, so she said, "This is nice. Fancy kind of safe house, isn't it?"

"No. It's mine."

What the hell? "Um, no. I agreed to be taken to a safe place, not—"

"This is a safe place."

"But it's your *house*. We were only shagging a few hours ago, and now I'm in your private space where it could happen again. No, I can't—"

"It won't be happening again any time soon. You're not in a good place emotionally. Mentally, either, I'd bet. You're going to look after yourself here until I can haul Jez's arse in, then you're going to move on to a better life." He paused. "Right?"

She sighed, asking herself why every damn thing had to be so difficult, why obstacles were always in her way for one reason or another. She could never just *be* these days, always wound up, waiting for the gavel that was Jez to come down on her and commit her to a life behind invisible bars.

Sod it. She'd give this a go, telling Kane everything she knew and suspected about Jez, then, once Jez was banged up, she was off. She had funds in a private account Jez didn't know about — that was why her credit card was constantly near its limit — and her statements and letters from her mum had been redirected to Henry's. She picked the mail up whenever she had coffee at his place. She'd been drawing cash out on credit and telling Jez she'd bought this or that, showing him old clothes still with tags on, ones he'd forgotten about. She had enough for a deposit on a new place, for a bit of furniture, some spends to keep her going for a while. Sixteen years salting cash away was a long time. She'd manage. There was employment to be had, at a supermarket or corner shop, the same as she'd had before he'd stopped her working.

Resigned to being caged in for a bit longer — it was a means to an end and well worth it — she got out of the car and waited for Kane to join her by the wooden front door. The modest house was nothing like she was used to these days, but it was a cross between that and the one she'd grown up in, so she'd possibly be more at ease here.

Kane collected her suitcase then opened the front door. He held his arm out as if silently saying *ladies first*, and she smiled at his gentlemanly behaviour. She could do with a man like him, but now wasn't the time to be thinking of another relationship. Rebounds were never good, so people said. She wouldn't know. She'd only ever been Jez's girlfriend.

She stood in the hallway, awkwardness squeezing her stomach, a little girl lost in a new world she wasn't sure she could fit into. She'd dreamed about it so many times, but to actually be here now, away from Jez, it didn't seem real.

"It'll take some getting used to," Kane said, shutting the door. He pushed her case, and it rolled off towards a door at the end. "But you can do this, you know. You're strong enough; otherwise, how did you go out tonight and do what you did?"

"What *we* did," she said. "I don't know, if I'm honest. It was a spur-of-the-moment thing. I'd had enough, and it was my way of taking some sort of control. And just think, if I hadn't gone, I'd still be there now, and so would Mrs Smithson."

"That isn't your fault. Mrs Smithson, I mean."

He took her hand and guided her to the far door, opening it and nudging her suitcase so it stood against the wall out of the way. She slipped her hand from his, and he raised his eyebrows for a fraction of a second then walked into the room. A kitchen, it was, similar to hers at home — *it isn't home anymore* — all gleaming white appliances, high-gloss cupboards in black, and a white table and chairs. She sat, not knowing what else to do, and waited for his interrogation about Jez and what he got up to.

"I don't know about you," he said, flicking the kettle on, "but I'm going to make us a cup of tea, then I'm off to bed."

Oh. Well. "Okay. I could do with some sleep myself."

But she'd be awake all night, she just knew it, tossing and turning in a strange bed, unable to get Jez out of her head, that blood on his temple, those scratches. Had he got them from Mrs Smithson when he'd killed her?

"Did you see the blood on him, those scratches?" she blurted.

"I did. You didn't see me talking to a uniformed officer after I put your case in the boot then?"

He did? "No."

"Jez will be taken in. That blood will be tested. We have the perfect excuse — Mrs Smithson. Those scratches will be swabbed. All right, he'll probably be let out after questioning — which I'll do in the morning, he deserves a night in the cells even if he didn't kill her — but if those results come back with DNA identified as belonging to Mrs Smithson, you won't be seeing him again."

"I don't plan on it anyway."

He made the tea then, and they sat in silence at the table, Kane opposite, one of his knees pressed against hers. It was nice, that feeling of someone good being there with her, so she didn't move her leg to break contact.

She finished her tea, and he popped the cups in the dishwasher, turned out the kitchen light, and hefted her case up the stairs. She went up after him, remembering how he'd felt earlier in the hotel room, his skin, his everything, then shook the thoughts away.

He showed her to one of his spare rooms, a double bed in the centre covered in a tasteful dove-grey duvet. Built-in wardrobes with sliding mirrored doors stood to the left, black cabinets either side of the bed to match the black leather headboard, all in all a room obviously decorated by a man.

He left her case by the door and retreated out onto the landing. "Try and get some sleep, all right?"

She nodded.

"I have to be at work by eight," he said. "So help yourself to food when you get up—or I might make you breakfast, depends how I'm strapped for time. Make yourself at home. Just don't go out for now, okay?"

She nodded again, and after he'd left and closed her door, the splash of a shower filtered through, and she moved to a second door in her room. She looked inside—an en suite—and decided to shower herself. She could do with

74

scrubbing that house off her, the home she'd been unhappy in for so long, even though she'd showered already tonight.

Sometimes it was the best thing to do, washing it all away.

NINE

Kane stared at Pickins across the table. The man really was a prick, like Kane had told Charlotte, and it seemed like days ago he'd been with her in that hotel room. So much had happened since that hour he'd spent with her in the pub and the next hour in bed. Pickins didn't deserve her. The fucker had a diamond and didn't even know it. Didn't care.

Richard Lemon sat beside Kane, whisky fumes coming off him, cigarette smoke lingering on his clothes. His shirt, stained at the armpits, looked hard and crusty there. Yellow from old sweat. If he had a wife, she'd be sick of the stench of him, but he'd never been married, and it didn't seem like he'd be waiting at the end of the aisle for some clueless bride in the future either. From what Richard had said, he spent most of his time outside of work up the boozer or acting out the role of potato on his couch, Johnnie in front of him whatever the scenario.

"What were you doing yesterday evening?" Kane asked Pickins.

"No comment." Pickins folded his arms across his chest and smirked, the grin almost lost inside his trendy beard and moustache.

"People who have something to hide tend to say that. So, I'll ask again. What were you doing yesterday evening?"

Pickins smiled wide, showing pristine teeth the same shape and size as Charlotte's. The pair had spent a fortune on dentistry, that much was obvious. "Well, it's like this, see. I was with my missus the whole time. Ask her, she'll vouch for me."

She bloody won't. "I'd like *you* to tell me what you did with your girlfriend."

Pickins chuckled. "What, you want me to tell you I fucked her up the arse, do you? Because that's what I did."

Kane held back a sigh—didn't clench his teeth. The muscles would flex in his jaw if he did, and Pickins would know he'd pissed him off. Got to him.

Blood boiling and threatening to force him to say something he shouldn't, Kane asked, "What else did you do?"

Pickins shook his head. "Blimey, you're a right kinky bastard, aren't you, wanting to know all the ins and outs. Did you like what I did there? Ins and outs…" He pressed a fingertip to his chin and rolled his eyes towards the pockmarked ceiling. Lowering them again to level his gaze on Kane, he said, "Now let's see. I fondled her tits for a bit, then I rubbed her—"

"You're clearly not interested in saving yourself," Kane said, reaching across to poise his finger over the stop button of the recording machine. "Interview suspended at—"

"Aww, wait. Just wait, will you? I'm messing around, aren't I. No need to get your Calvin's in a twist." Pickins unfolded his arms and propped his elbows on the table. Rubbed his palms over his face. Breathed out through the gap where his pinkies almost met. "Look," he said, voice muffled behind his hands. He dropped them to his lap. "I was out, all right? Out at the time that old dear died."

"Where?"

He cast his eyes down then back up to stare at Kane. "If I told you, I'd have to kill you."

He roared with laughter, head thrown back, the front chair legs rising, him balancing there, and all Kane needed to do was push him a bit and Pickins would slam onto the floor, whacking his head on the radiator behind. But there were cameras, and he didn't need the hassle he'd have over one momentary lapse into red-mist anger.

"This is serious, Pickins," Kane said.

"I know, copper. I *was* being serious."

A threat then, one Kane was glad had been recorded.

Richard farted.

For fuck's sake!

Kane flared his nostrils. "So, you're not going to tell us what you were doing, is that right?"

"I just did. I was fucking my —"

"Your *missus* doesn't have the same story as you."

"Then she's lying." Pickins lowered the chair and rested his forearms on the table.

They sat in silence for a full minute, Kane waiting for the second hand to tick round just a bit more than that to ramp up the tension. And the room was full of it, oozing out of Pickins as though tangible, something Kane could reach out and grab and shove down the bastard's throat, choking him. Richard wasn't successful in hiding another gaseous expulsion, a burp this time, and Kane's patience was pushed to the limit. If he didn't get out of there and away from the pisshead beside him and the arsehole in front of him, he might not be able to control himself.

"We'll take a break." Kane said the necessary for the benefit of the tape then rose.

Richard stood, too, going out to ask a couple of officers to escort Pickins to his cell, hopefully. Pickins sat there inspecting his fingernails—no thick oil beneath them, what with it being scraped out earlier to go off for testing, just a faint line remaining now. Kane had made an important phone call once he'd had the samples in hand, and with any luck, by the end of the morning, he'd know whether Pickins had killed Mrs Smithson.

"I want a fag before you lock me up," Pickins said.

Kane ignored him and waited by the door until the officers came, then he left, steaming down the corridor, up three flights of stairs, and into his office without checking on his team in the incident room. He wasn't fit to speak to anyone at the moment.

He sat behind his desk and went through everything in his head.

Pickins had been out, Charlotte had said he'd left before she had, so his tale about being home all night was bollocks. She'd been gone for the two hours they'd spent together, plus the time it had taken for her to walk to the pub and for Kane to drive her home, so two hours forty minutes max.

Pickins had been home when Charlotte had arrived, but with no one saying they'd seen him come back—Kane had checked all the neighbours' statements earlier that morning— there was no telling how long he'd actually been out for. Long enough to kill Mrs Smithson? It didn't take but a minute or so to whack someone on the back of the head and push them onto a bonfire, so he could have done that on his way home, gone in his own house, and no one would be any the wiser.

Last night, Pickins had given a brief statement at his front door to a uniform, saying he hadn't seen anything out of the ordinary, and the officer had taken it at face value—probably new to the force and unaware of just who Pickins was.

So he'd been home at nine or thereabouts to have been questioned. Where had he been before that? And where had he gone afterwards? Kane had dropped Charlotte off at about nine-forty, and she'd said Pickins had pissed off out again around ten. The street had been pretty busy, everyone having a good old nose, and Kane had turned up at Charlotte's shortly after. Her story about her life had taken an hour or so in the telling, then Pickins had come back, just after the pubs kicked out. He hadn't smelt of alcohol at the front door, though.

Pickins could have done it, there wasn't a question mark hanging in the air about that, but what if the blood wasn't Mrs Smithson's? What if the scratches had been made by someone else?

If so, who?

Kane kicked the bin by his desk, sending the screwed-up papers and empty vending machine cups flying. Dregs of coffee seeped out of two of them, forming penny-sized domes of liquid on the carpet. He didn't bother clearing up the mess and instead flung himself out of his chair to look through the window.

Victoria Road below, congested with traffic, one car snorting black fumes out of its exhaust pipe—*he should get a ticket for that*—gave Kane the urge to pack up and bugger off on holiday. Someplace where the air was clean, and everyone walked instead of driving. Where people didn't spend their final seconds of life burning in a back garden they used to drink their first cuppa of a summer morning in, soaking up the sounds of birds in the trees, the bees coming out to collect pollen. Where kids didn't go to Pickins, hoping to buy the magic elixir to shoot into their veins, or smoke, or pop a pill, anything, something to take away the craving of addiction.

This world was fucked up, wasn't it? Totally and utterly fucked up.

He left his office, hating the feeling of not being able to do a damn thing about it all, and chatted with his team, added info to the whiteboard, and caught up on anything they'd come up with so far this morning. Nothing new. No one had seen anyone go to Mrs Smithson's prior to her death, and the neighbour directly beside her had only gone inside her house to check she was okay because the front door had been gaping open as he'd walked past on his way home from work.

The man, Fred Hill, a forty-something gym owner, had gone into her back garden, seen what he'd thought was someone on the bonfire, then rushed out to the front shouting for help. Returning inside, he'd grabbed a washing-up bowl, tipping the dirty contents of plates and cups into the sink, and filled it with water to toss it on the flames.

By then, a Mick Drake had arrived on the scene and, upon going into the back garden, had spotted a hose. He'd turned the spigot and jetted water onto the bonfire while Fred continued to dash in and out with bowls.

Delia Robson had called the ambulance and police, then had waited on the pavement outside Mrs Smithson's house to direct them where to go.

All this Kane had gleaned from the statements, and he set his team the task of sifting through them all again to see if there were any inconsistencies. He turned to Richard, who sat in his chair with his head back and eyes closed, a snore trumpeting out of him, jolting him awake.

"Keeping you up, are we?" Kane asked, going over to sit on the edge of his desk. "Late night, was it?"

Richard blinked, bleary-eyed, and stared as though he had no idea who Kane was.

"What's the *matter* with you?" Kane said quietly. "Do you need some time off?"

"No," Richard said, scooting his chair forward and waking his monitor up with the shake of the mouse. "I'm good."

If you say so. "Well, I'd ask you to come with me to have another crack at Pickins, but the state you're in, I don't —"

The faint ringing of his office phone shut him up, and he strode in there, hoping it was Charlotte, then gave himself a stern talking to for even entertaining that.

He lifted the phone out of the dock. "DI Barnett." Held his breath. It was her, wasn't it, not knowing what to say now he'd picked up?

"Vic Atkins on the front desk, sir."

Fucking hell.

"Yep?" Kane squatted to clear up the mess he'd made, the toe of his shoe obscuring one of the wet splotches that hadn't even soaked into the carpet yet.

"You're needed down at the warehouses round the back of Clarks, sir."

Had a drug addict camping out there taken some dodgy gear? Kane's spirits lifted, macabre as that was. If that was what had gone down, and the user could identify Pickins as his supplier… It couldn't be that easy, could it? Pickins employed runners, no way he'd get his own hands dirty — except with oil, that was.

"For what, Vic?" he asked.

"There's a body there, sir. Young sex worker, late twenties. Suffocated apparently. Got a bit of a broken nose."

How can a nose be a 'bit' broken?

"Go on."

"Gilbert's there now. Found by that homeless fella, the one who always walks round town with a shopping trolley. Can't think of his bloody name."

"Old Bill, funny enough. Beats me why that didn't stick in your head, considering what you do for a living." Kane righted the bin and stood.

"That's the fella. Anyway, the poor bloke had a funny turn. He's down at Horley General now in case you need to speak to him."

"Right. I'll go to the scene first. Tarra." He ended the call then jabbed speed dial one for the chief. "Uh, it's me, Kane, sir. There's been another murder."

"Christ Almighty. Okie dokie, keep me in the loop when you get the chance. With last night's as well, you'll be swamped, so just a couple of minutes for an update will do. Say tomorrow afternoon?"

"Yes, sir. Catch you then."

He hung up, chucked the phone on the desk. It skidded to a halt against a stack of mail. Feeling defeated, he went in search of Richard, envying the chief for being able to stay in his office all day.

Richard stood in front of the water cooler, seemingly mesmerised by the trickle going into the white plastic cup.

"Come on," Kane said. "We've got work to do."

Richard jumped, and water poured over the rim of the cup and into the grate below.

Kane flicked the stream off and frowned. "What the *hell* is your problem?"

"What's on the agenda?" Richard asked, his change of subject, yet again, pissing Kane off something chronic.

"Murder of a sex worker," Kane said.

"Aww, fuck's sake. You *know* how much I hate prossers." His moustache wavered from the breath he huffed out.

"Hate them or not, they exist, and we have a job to do. Have you never wondered why they have to sell sex? That life might have kicked them in the damn teeth so they had no choice but to turn to the oldest profession in the book? Or because drugs, sold by people like Pickins, forced them to make money — and lots of it — fast? You have no idea what those women have been through, so keep your opinions to yourself and get your arse into gear."

Or I'm telling the chief you're a waste of sodding space and should be put out to pasture.

Kane stalked off, the sound of Richard shuffling behind him, huffing and puffing, setting his teeth on edge. In the car park at the rear of the station, Kane waited in his Fiat for Richard to catch up, dreading the moment the man sat beside him and stunk out the enclosed space.

Richard got in, not bothering with his seat belt, and Kane drove off, his mind switching between two people: Mrs Smithson and the sex worker.

Then another female.
Charlotte.
Damn it.

TEN

Charlotte wandered around for the umpteenth time, bored out of her skull and, oddly, wishing she was at home. At least she knew where everything was in her own place. There was nothing like your personal space, was there, and even though she'd longed to get away from it, now she wasn't there, it called to her, a mournful cry inside her to come back, to use the Dyson on the beautiful carpets, the Mr Sheen on the dining room table, her buffing it with a pink microfibre cloth.

She set about cleaning Kane's house instead of imagining doing hers. Although obsessively tidy, the rooms had too much dust on the surfaces — all right, only a slight layer, but she could still see it, so it had to go. She spent a good hour using elbow grease to bring everything up sparkling, but by nine-thirty she was finished and bored.

In her room, she switched her phone on, dreading having messages waiting from Jez, but only one from Henry sat there, the first line visible in the oblong text box. She clicked it.

POST HAS ARRIVED. BANK STATEMENT BY THE LOOKS OF IT, AND ONE FROM YOUR MUM.

She sent a reply.

OKAY, CAN I NIP OVER IN ABOUT FIFTEEN MINUTES?

Might be better if he thought she was still at home.

YES, THAT'S FINE. SEE YOU THEN. I'LL GET THE KETTLE ON.

She rang for a taxi — one of the few numbers in her contact list approved by Jez — while slipping on her boots, then went downstairs with her handbag — *shit, my bra's still in it* — and found a spare set of keys on a hook on the inside of one of the kitchen cupboards. She'd noticed them last night when Kane had taken the cups out to make their tea. Checking the keys one by one in the front door, pleased that a dull, gold Yale fitted, she slid the bunch into her bag then went out to wait at the kerb for the cab.

She thought about Kane telling her to stay indoors, but getting a letter from her mum seemed more important than keeping safe somehow. Stupid, but she couldn't help herself.

The taxi arrived within a minute, and in no time she was in her old street, nervous on the pavement in case Jez hadn't been collared for the blood and scratches last night after all and he'd see her. Head down, she scuttled along, stomach in knots, her heart beating so hard her chest ached. At Henry's, she looked over at the home she'd shared with Jez, expecting him to be standing between the lions again, but he wasn't there.

She pushed the gate inwards and rushed to press Henry's bell. Its *ding-dong* echoed, and then his shape appeared behind the misted glass, and he opened the door, all smiles. His moustache swept up at the ends, a furry banana, hair yellowing on the tips and coming through grey near the roots. An almost spent roll-up hung on his bottom lip, smoke writhing upwards and into one of his eyes, and he squinted. Head to toe in black, he was, his usual preference — jumper, jeans, socks — his dark eyes showing his kindness and honesty.

"Come on, come on," he said, moving back so she could step in.

She went into the living room as if she lived there, comfortable in his house the same as always, and sat in her usual spot on the brown sofa. She took her boots off then tucked her feet up, placed one of the pale pink cushions against the arm of the sofa, and propped her elbow on it.

Henry stood in the doorway. "What about Mrs Smithson, eh? Fuck me. Give me two seconds, and I'll bring the coffee in. We can talk about it, then you can tell me what you've been up to, all right?"

She smiled, and he disappeared, coming back a minute or so later with a tray bearing two cups, a plate of chocolate Hobnob biscuits, and her letters. He placed it on the coffee table, and she reached forward to scoop up her mail.

"Thanks, you know how much I appreciate you doing this for me." She opened her bag just a little and eased the letters through the centimetre gap, conscious Henry might spot her cerise bra. Bag on the floor in front of her, she reached for her coffee. He always put it in a cup he'd bought especially for her, pink, KEEP CALM, I'M A PRINCESS written on the side in white with a crown at the top. *A queen to Jez and a princess to me, love!* She cradled it in her hands. Maybe she'd have a biscuit in a bit. Kane had left her bacon and sausages this morning, so she wasn't peckish yet.

"You're more than welcome, love, you know that." He sat in one of the chairs of the three-piece suite, placing a messy scribble of tobacco on a Rizla, rolling it into a fag then licking the gum to secure it. "Bloody bad business going on round here, eh?" He tilted his head towards the window. "Can't say I'll miss her bonfires, though."

"They *were* a bit much, weren't they? Still, I'll miss seeing her standing by her gate. I'm sure she did that because she was lonely. You know, she waited until someone came along so she could have a natter. Can't have been nice for her if she felt alone most of the time."

"No, but you get on with it, don't you," he said. "Take me, for instance. On my own at fifty-nine — not any age, is it, fifty-nine — waiting for the right girl to notice me, but I manage. If I had a wife — not that I want one, mind — maybe it wouldn't be so bad, but you know I prefer living by myself, although a girlfriend would be all right staying over sometimes." He chuckled. Roll-up parked between his lips, he lit it with a match, inhaled, then blew out a blue-grey tornado-like funnel of smoke.

Charlotte didn't mind. She was used to Jez smoking his Superkings, and besides, Henry's brand of tobacco didn't smell the same. It was sweet. A chill rippled down her spine at the thought of Jez, and she pushed him to the back of her mind. Hopefully he was in the nick by now, where he couldn't do anything except piss off the police. Still, it was bloody horrible being in this street so soon after she'd got out of it.

I won't stay long. I need to get out of here as soon as possible without it seeming off to Henry.

"I saw your Jez being carted off in a cop car last night after you left with some bloke in a suit," he said. "What was that all about, eh?"

So much for not thinking about that bastard. "Oh, he was being awkward about his whereabouts last night," she lied. "So they took him down the station to get a statement out of him."

"Where did you go, though?" He sucked on his fag. Smoke billowed with each word, "Who did *you* go off with?"

What do I say now? "I was out, you know, getting some milk, so it looked like I might have killed Mrs—"

"*Killed*, you say? What do you mean *killed*?" He coughed, the smoke most probably getting caught in his throat.

Charlotte knew how he must feel. She'd been just as staggered by the fact Mrs Smithson had been murdered. She was too conscious by half that she'd let the cat out of the bag and didn't know what the hell to say to patch up the mess she'd made. "Oh, well, I assume she was killed, otherwise, why would they take us down to the station? I had to go down as well, see. They kept asking where I was, over and over, like they didn't believe I'd just nipped out to the shop. They said they'll be checking the CCTV there, but that's all right, they'll see me on it and know I was telling the truth."

"But what about the suitcase?" he asked.

"The suitcase?"

"Yes, that plain-clothed copper put one in the boot."

"Oh, for some reason, he wanted the clothes I'd had on last night when I went to the shop. I didn't have a carrier bag or anything so I shoved them in a suitcase."

The trouble with lies was, you ended up digging a deeper hole for yourself the longer the tale went on. She should have just gone with the account Kane had concocted, but it was too late now. She'd said what she'd said, and she didn't think she ought to change her story in case Henry viewed her in a different light and didn't want to be her friend anymore. She'd grown fond of him, enough to want to still pop here, or maybe meet him at a coffee shop sometime in the future — if she stuck around this town, that was.

"So you were only just let out then, were you? This morning?" he asked, jabbing his fag into an ashtray then picking up his drink.

"Yes, thought I'd come to see you first before I go home." That didn't sound plausible. If she loved Jez, she'd want to go straight home to see if he was back yet, and she hadn't. But at least this way she could find out if he was in their house now.

"I see." Henry sipped his coffee. "Haven't seen him arrive, and trust me, I'd know. I've been standing at the window all morning. Wanted to keep abreast of what's happening. The police are still there, in her garden. Saw them bring her out on a stretcher first thing. Better than watching *Coronation Street*, know what I mean?"

She didn't find that funny. "Yes, it's been a strange few hours." Hadn't it just. This time yesterday morning, she'd been sick to death of being caged up indoors, and her rebellious plan to go out had been born while she'd scoured the oven on her hands and knees. She'd realised she was a drudge, constantly doing housework to pass the time, or cooking elaborate meals Jez wouldn't even eat because he wasn't home much. A Cinderella, her glass slipper well and truly in the past, gathering dust in a forgotten corner, her knight in shining armour an illusion, something she'd wanted to see him as, something he'd not turned out to be.

"So Jez didn't mind you going out for milk, then?" he asked and swept up a Hobnob. Some crumbs fell off it onto his top. "Unusual, that is. Times past, you've told me he can't abide you leaving the house unless it's to come and see me."

"Yes, well, he doesn't like not having milk for his coffee in the mornings, so rather than have him bite my head off or whatever, I thought it best to go. I ended up not buying it anyway. Heard people talking about the trouble in the street."

"That was quick," he said. "News travelling on the grapevine, I mean. Shop's only a minute or two down there." He curved his thumb and jabbed it towards the window. "So was Mrs Smithson's door open when you went past like I heard it was?"

She blushed at the canny way he had of sniffing out inconsistencies. It was true, the shop was only a couple of streets away, so Mrs Smithson would have already been dead when I'd walked on my fictitious journey for the news to reach the shop that quickly. *Bloody hell…* "I didn't notice whether it was open or not."

"Well, it most likely would have been by then if people were gassing about it at the till. And you'd have seen people in the street, surely."

She shrugged. "I don't know. Maybe I got mixed up. I'm tired from being at the police station all night."

"Bit odd that they kept you overnight, isn't it?" He chomped on his biscuit.

It crunched like Jez's gherkins.

His questions were getting on her nerves— she'd never felt this way when he'd probed in the past. But in the past, she hadn't lied to him, and she acknowledged she was more annoyed at herself for bullshitting him than anything else.

"It is what it is," she said and grabbed a biscuit, taking small bites, thinking she'd better leave once she'd finished it, put some distance between them if he was in an inquisitive mood. She felt for him. Being alone most of the time, it stood to reason he'd chat the hind legs off a donkey whenever anyone dropped by for a visit. She'd been just as bad, nattering away to him on her previous visits, telling him too much. Things Jez wouldn't approve of if he found out she'd blabbed.

"I've made you uncomfortable, love," Henry said, biscuit eaten while she'd been thinking. "I didn't mean any harm. Sometimes I forget and turn into a bit of a detective. All those crime shows I watch, I suppose, giving me ideas. Silly bastard, me."

He smiled, and not for the first time, she saw him not as his age, but a good-looking older man who must have turned a few heads when he'd been younger. He was almost a silver fox now, and it was a shame his smoking had turned his moustache mustard. She imagined what he'd look like without it.

Nice.

"It's all right," she said. "I'm used to you after all these years."

"It's been a while that we've known each other, hasn't it? I must say, you're looking nice today. More like your old self."

"Hmm. I got stuck in a rut. Thought I'd best dig myself out of it. I'm thirty-odd, not sixty."

"Hey, less of the age bashing. I'm coming up to sixty, don't forget."

"Doesn't seem like it. If it wasn't for you going grey"—she gave him a cheeky grin—"I'd say you were much younger."

"Good job I know you mean well. You can go off people, you know."

She laughed, thankful they were back to normal again, him not asking uncomfortable questions and her not having to lie. She finished her biscuit, downed her coffee, then popped her boots on while he rolled another ciggie. "I'd better go. Can I borrow your loo?"

"Can't you wait until you get home or something?" he asked.

Damn. "Um…no." She winked. "I'm bursting."

"Go on, off you go."

She left the room, using the small loo beside the front door, washed her hands, then returned to the living room to collect her bag. "I'll be off now."

Henry stood and held his arms out. "Give us a hug then."

She cuddled him like she always did, feeling safe in his arms, cared for. He squeezed then let her go, moving out into the hallway. She followed, and he opened the door.

"See you soon," he said.

"Okay. Bye for now."

She walked down the path, and the door clicked closed at the same time she latched his gate. Needing to keep up the charade now she'd started it, suspecting Henry would be watching from the window, she crossed the street and strode up her old path, the gravel shifting beneath her weight, her feet almost going from under her.

Please don't let him be back.

She slid her hand in her bag and foraged about for her keys, pulling Kane's out the first time then found her own. Key in the lock, she turned it, all the while shitting bricks in case Jez was home. Surely he wouldn't be, not at around tennish, the time she guessed it to be. Kane said he'd be interviewing him this morning, so she might get lucky.

Inside — *what the fuck am I doing here?* — she shut the door and, without looking up the stairs or in the living room, she bolted through the kitchen, unlocked and opened the back door, and stepped into the garden. Had it only been a few short hours ago she'd sat out here with Kane, spilling her guts?

You shouldn't have done that.

She bit that pointing finger of a thought off at the second knuckle and forged ahead to the bottom of the garden. At the gate, she peered through a knothole into the street behind and, as no one was about, she left the garden and walked at a quick pace while digging in her bag for her phone. She dialled the same taxi firm, asking to be picked up at the end of the road, and waited there beneath a streetlight, the plastic casing broken, the hole in it resembling a gunshot through glass and revealing the bulb within. After five minutes of her anxiously tapping her foot, she released a sigh of relief as the cab swept up to her, and she got in, giving Kane's address.

Someone tapped on the driver's-side window, a man with a hipster beard like Jez's. For a moment she thought it *was* him, but this bloke had a blond fade cut and a jacket and trousers on, and he was barely twenty if she was any judge. Jez wouldn't wear clothes like that. For working in the garage, it was an orange boiler suit, and at night, for the pub, black jeans and white T-shirts, maybe his hoodie.

The cabbie opened the window. "Sorry, mate, just picked up a fare."

"I'm in a rush. I need... My mum's had a heart attack."

Charlotte thought of *her* mum, who she hadn't seen since she'd moved in with Jez, and how she'd feel if she got that sort of news. "It's all right. Let him get in."

The man peered into the back. "Thank you. You're an absolute legend." He ran around the front of the taxi and threw himself into the back seat beside her, knocking her bag into the spacious footwell. She moved to get it, but he got there first, his fingers brushing hers. She jolted, worried Jez would come leaping through the gate and spot her, thinking she was running off with someone else.

"I've got it," he said.

She turned away, embarrassed by the blush heating her face and, while he put her bag on the seat between them, she gazed out of the side window and said to the cabbie, "Take him first. He needs to get home before me."

The driver got there quickly, and after the man had thanked her again, he raced up a garden path and hammered on the door with the side of his fist. She hoped his mum would be okay.

I badly need to see mine, but reading her letter will have to do.

Kane only lived around the corner from here. Once at his, she rushed inside, hung his keys back in the cupboard, then went to her room to open the envelope she looked forward to every single week.

ELEVEN

English was boring. Debbie preferred maths or chemistry, something that taxed her brain more, something she could understand. The teacher reading *Hamlet*, her voice a monotonous drone, had Debbie's eyelids drooping. She'd spent much of last night awake, thinking about her visit to his house that evening. She could hardly stand the tension, butterflies exploding in her tummy every time he popped into her head. God, he was gorgeous. Her friends would go *eww* and fake-vomit if they knew she fancied him, so she'd kept it to herself all this time. Why reveal who she had her eye on if all they'd do was take the piss out of her for it? Anyway, it was delicious keeping a secret. Made it all the more exciting. And she liked excitement, planned on having lots of it once she'd convinced him she belonged in his bed.

He wouldn't say no, would he? Toss her offer back at her? No, she'd seen how he'd looked at her recently, when she'd walked by his house on her way to school and he'd been at the open door talking to some kid she vaguely remembered as being in year eleven when she'd been in seven. She'd wondered what he was doing there, the kid, until the man of her fantasies had given him a package and the kid had driven off.

A courier, that's what he was.

"Pay attention, Deborah," Miss Boring as Fuck said.

Debbie jolted, her eyes widening, the tiredness vanishing. Titters erupted, although Miss didn't appear amused. She glared at Debbie, eyes massive behind her thick lenses, the black frames shaped like some woman's specs from the forties. Young, about thirty or so,

Miss loved Shakespeare more than she loved tending to her appearance. Clearly.

Flushing at her spiteful thought—and she'd bet Miss would think she was embarrassed at being caught half asleep—Debbie scanned the page to catch up to where Miss now carried on reading, wishing this lesson would end so she could skive biology—more about blood cells today, ugh—and sneak a crafty fag somewhere so she could think about what she'd wear later.

Mum and Dad wouldn't bat an eye at her leaving the house in a short skirt or whatever. She'd opted for that sort of thing for a while now, hoping she'd catch his attention. Seemed she had if he wanted her over at his house. Her plan had worked, and she wanted to laugh at how everything was coming together, pleased at herself for using similar tactics she'd seen on some soap or other. Might have been *Eastenders*.

The bell clanged, and she scrabbled from her seat, gathering her book and bag then barging out of the room. Someone called her name, but she didn't bother to turn to see who it was. She wanted out of there for the next fifty minutes, and she'd make out, if she was questioned as to where she'd been, that she'd got stuck on the loo with stomach trouble. She hadn't used that excuse for a while, so it'd fly, she reckoned.

As she slipped through the hole in the wire fence at the bottom of the school field, she smiled at the thought of losing her virginity tonight. If she played this right, she'd be a woman come the morning, and he'd be her boyfriend *and*, if she continued to get lucky, her husband in a couple of years. She'd only live a few doors away from Mum and Dad then, and after they'd got over the shock of who she'd chosen to be with, they'd come round for Sunday dinner maybe, play with the grandkids.

Fucking excellent.

TWELVE

Jez was fucked off. Since he'd been spoken to by that bloody copper who'd taken Charlotte off last night, his stinky sidekick gassing up the room, Jez had been stuck in a cell. He'd found himself in one plenty of times before in his younger years— disorderly conduct, beating up blokes when he'd gulped back too much voddy, that kind of thing—so it wouldn't usually bother him, but he had a meeting today with some young lad who'd said he could shift a shed load of weed and a few bags of coke inside a week. It was switch-over day, the dough for the product, and if he wasn't out of here by three o'clock, getting to their agreed location by four, the deal could be well and truly buggered. He had to pick up that product beforehand, too. He wasn't stupid enough to keep it at his own place, but the person holding it for him didn't live a million miles away, so he wouldn't fret about that.

His mind wandered.

Where was Charlotte? It pissed him off big time that he didn't know. He couldn't even check the app on his phone to snoop at her location. The sergeant on the desk had put it inside a clear bag with Jez's Rolex and wallet last night. DI Barnett had another think coming if he thought Jez wouldn't be able to work out where she'd gone. Jez had been tracking her whereabouts for a few years now, but the only thing with that app was it worked in real time, didn't store previous locations. Last night, with the murder and everything, he'd forgotten to log in to see if she was at the shop like Cobbings had said.

Jez knew enough about the law to know he'd be allowed out soon, asked not to leave town or the country — *blah blah effing blah* — while they processed the blood and the swabs from those scratches. He stewed about that, irritated he hadn't cleaned himself up properly, but he hadn't expected to find a copper in his house when he'd got home, had he.

And as for Charlotte getting a threatening letter. That was just bollocks.

Anyway, he wasn't going to think about that side of things anymore, so he stretched out on the narrow bench with a plastic-covered pad the depth of a Tesco's triple sandwich on it and tucked his hands behind his head. Might as well get a bit of shut-eye while he could. He'd been awake all night, some drunk bastard hollering then puking all over the shop, going by the sound of the splash, so now it was quiet, he stood a better chance of getting some kip.

He breathed deeply through his nose then released it out of his mouth. Good technique, that, for calming the old nerves. Just as he was nodding off, he remembered that Kane Barnett, the wanker, hadn't sent anyone to let Jez out for a fag break—unless he wasn't allowed his smoker's rights anymore—and rage seared through him all over again.

Once he'd sorted the drug deal, he'd have to find something to take his anger out on, because it wasn't like Charlotte was home to bear the brunt, was it?

Fucking bitch.

THIRTEEN

The inside of the warehouse on the ground floor wasn't too bad in terms of litter, but every room on the second floor except the one the body was in appeared as if someone had come in with black bags from their kitchen bin and dumped it all out. Surprised no rats scuttled around in search of food—or maybe they'd run off owing to the human activity—Kane went back into the only room with a door, his inspection of the others complete. He didn't envy the guys having to take all that rubbish away to sift through later.

Gilbert was packing up his bag, his face drawn, as though he hadn't had much sleep last night. Richard stood in the corner to the right, smoking a goddamn cigarette.

"Put that out," Kane snapped. Jesus Christ, what was the bloody matter with the man? "Downstairs, not in this building."

Richard moseyed forward, sighing, an inch-long cylinder of ash dropping off his fag and landing by Kane's foot, thankfully still intact so Kane could scoop it into a baggie so it didn't contaminate the scene.

With Richard gone, Kane said to Gilbert, voice low so the SOCOs in the room didn't hear, "Do you know what's up with him?"

Gilbert zipped his bag closed. "No idea, mate. Ask him, why don't you? But something's not right, I'll give you that. He's been behaving weirder than usual lately. Not with it, like he's got something on his mind."

"Probably whisky," Kane muttered.

Gilbert laughed. "Yeah, it wouldn't surprise me. He stinks like a distillery, that one. From the amount he smokes and drinks, I can guarantee his lungs and liver aren't pretty. Pity the poor sod who does his postmortem. Let's hope it isn't me, eh?"

"It might well be," Kane said. "He'll drink himself to death before long. And I agree—he looks like he's got the weight of the world on his shoulders, like something's troubling him."

"The only thing that would trouble Richard is if Sainsbury's runs out of Johnnie Walker and Lambert and Butler." Gilbert sighed. "Right, back to work matters. From her temperature"—he pointed at the victim—"we're talking death occurring late last night, before midnight. She's not in rigor, so that corroborates my estimate—she's been stiff and limped out again. She was suffocated. See the hand print there? The finger marks on her cheek, the thumb just below her jaw?"

"Suffocated with a hand? Fuck me…" Kane swallowed. What possessed these people?

"Probably a disgruntled punter." Gilbert shrugged. "She's had her ear chewed on and all, poor cow."

Kane shook his head.

"You've got to hope the DNA from her having sex brings back results of people already in the database." Gilbert smiled. "Otherwise, you're fucked."

"Thanks for that."

Gilbert chortled. "Right. I'm just about to get her down to my little sanctuary for the dead, so if you want to have a shufti at her, do it now. And don't be too long about it. I'm hangry — great word that, don't you think? Didn't have a chance to eat breakfast before I was called out."

Kane moved closer to the woman, and something blue and plastic caught his attention beside her hand. "Pick that up for me, will you?"

Gilbert *tsked*. "I asked you to do that a while back, Simon."

Simon, a SOCO, came over, pointed at the item, and Kane nodded. Simon used large tweezers to lift the piece and held it in front of Kane's face. A dolphin, cheap-looking, something you'd find on a bits-and-bobs stall at a market, nestled in a basket, lost among all the other under-a-quid crap in there. It had a circle on the curve of the dorsal fin, a ring doughnut type thing, where it had once hung on a necklace, a keyring, something like that. Could it have been in the room beforehand? He was inclined to think not — this room was too clean of anything bar a lump of concrete, the floor swept, and why *was* that when all the others were so filthy? If a tramp had cleaned it up to live here, some form of human life would be visible, wouldn't it? A crushed pop can, a sandwich wrapper, whatever. All right, the homeless tended to cart all their belongings with them, so he could understand why a sleeping bag or blanket wasn't rolled up in the corner, but…

Kane thanked Simon, who bagged the dolphin then continued with what he'd been doing prior to Kane interrupting him—on his hands and knees searching for evidence he wasn't likely to find.

Crouching, Kane peered at the victim's neck for signs of a necklace having been there, for evidence of it being ripped off, but the only thing on her throat was a dark brown mole the diameter of a thumbtack. He frowned.

"If you're looking for where that dolphin came from," Gilbert said, "try looking at her right wrist. Bracelet, I imagine. Got a few scratch marks."

Kane studied it. Gilbert was usually right, so Kane had no reason to doubt him. So she'd had a bracelet on—well, where was it? "Did you check beneath her yet?"

"Err, yes. What do you take me for, Barnett?" Gilbert came to stand beside him, grinning. "She had no ID on her, by the way, so you're fucked again."

"You have one hell of a warped sense of humour," Kane said. He sighed. He'd have to send two of his team out, the women would be better, to have a chat with the local sex workers to see if anyone recognised her description. Not that he could tell what she'd looked like in life. Her face was a wreck, puffy, a split lip, her nose skewed to one side, skin a terrible purple, a prestorm colour, the bellies of heavy clouds laden with rain.

"Finished?" Gilbert asked. "Or are you going to stand there and wait for her to reanimate and tell you who did it?" He laughed—hard and from the depths of his belly—and wiped a tear from below his eye. "Should have been a stand-up comic, me."

Kane shook his head. "Seriously, mate, don't give up your day job. See you later." He walked out, leaving Gilbert and company to the task of dealing with that poor woman's body.

Down the stairs, across the open space of the ground floor swarming with SOCOs, then outside to remove his white suit and gloves, Kane loosed an unsteady breath. He bundled the clothing up and walked to his car, dumping it on the back seat. Richard's familiar aroma wafted out, and Kane gritted his teeth. He couldn't go on working with him. He was next to useless, continually struggling through a hangover from being three sheets to the sodding wind the night before.

Kane got in the car, one foot in, one out, and stared across at Richard. A hip flask, wedged between Richard's inner thighs, the lid off, sent Kane to that place where he tended to say things he'd regret later.

"You," he said, snatching the flask then tossing it out of his open door, "need to sort yourself out. Nine times out of ten you're still pissed when you roll up at work, and when you're *at* work, you're not much good to anyone, in a daze, not listening, lounging about in the corner of crime scenes *smoking*. What the hell were you *doing*, you useless piece of *shit*?"

Richard didn't face him, vacantly staring through the windshield instead. His cheeks, red as usual, flared darker, and his eyes, glassy, gave Kane the sense the lights were on but nobody was home.

"Richard?"

"What?" he snapped. "Get off my back, will you? I've got an important thing going on later, and I need to get myself in the right frame of mind. You up my arsehole isn't helping. When you're in this sort of mood, you'd argue with a signpost. Now shut your bloody mouth and leave me alone."

Kane wanted to lay him out, but he wouldn't. He drew his leg inside the car, slammed the door, then sped away, curving sharply round corners—that'd teach the man to drink on the job, but if he was sick in Kane's car…

He headed for the station, foregoing visiting Old Bill in the hospital—someone else could do that. Kane doubted he'd get anything useful out of him anyway. Bill was usually half cut like Richard, using donations from his begging sessions to buy copious amounts of cheap beer from the off-licence.

The journey made in silence, apart from the occasional belch from Richard, meant for a tense few minutes. At the station, Kane parked and waited for Richard to vacate. Then he took the Febreze from his glove box, spraying liberal amounts until the smell of Richard had gone.

Once in his office, Kane slumped in his chair, drinking a Fanta orange from a multipack he kept in his desk drawer. He no longer gave a toss what Richard was doing—napping at his desk, boozing in the toilet, have at it, mate— preferring to get his thoughts in order instead. He pushed himself out of his seat, ants in his pants, and walked into the incident room.

His team worked at their desks, computer monitors filled with information. No one glanced up as he marched to the whiteboard and added the sex worker's information. Done, he turned to address them.

"Listen up. Another murder. Sex worker, suffocated by someone's hand. Nada and Erica, you two can go home now to get some rest because I want you out tonight questioning the women on the road opposite Clarks in town. Get there for seven, stay until you've asked everyone if one of them who's usually there, isn't. Hang around until after ten—some don't come out until their kids are in bed. Alistair, I want you down at the hospital now—stop what you're doing and *listen* to me, will you? *Jesus.*" Kane was of a mind to swing for someone. He was conducting without an orchestra here. "Find out where Old Bill is, the ward or whatever, and take a statement. He found the victim. Lara and Tim, keep sifting through last night's statements regarding Mrs Smithson. Richard…" Richard wasn't in the room. "Well, Richard can do what the fuck he likes. Why change a habit of a lifetime, eh? Okay, on you go. Let's get some damn results here, all right?"

He stalked over to the door, kicking it open, incensed that Richard was off God knew where. How was Kane meant to work with a partner like that? The last couple of years, Richard had got worse, and Kane wasn't putting up with it anymore. He'd be better off with Nada by his side. She was a good worker and didn't mind pulling double shifts.

Down the corridor, he knocked on the chief's door, the plaque gold with black writing: DCI OLIVER WINTER. Kane waited, the chief's voice a mumble through the wood—probably on the phone—then leant against the wall opposite, taking a breather to calm himself. Sensible that he did. He couldn't go in there, mad as a tormented rattler, hissing venom about Richard.

"Come in!"

119

Kane pushed off the wall, took a deep breath, and turned the handle. He stepped inside, and Winter's face told a story—he was harassed and livid about it, and Kane suspected the last thing the chief needed was him in here chapping his arse.

"Take a seat, Kane. Thought we had our chat scheduled for tomorrow?"

Kane all but fell into the chair, exhausted by his anger. "We did, but I need to talk to you about something—not the cases."

"Want a coffee?" Winter stood then walked military-style to his filing cabinet and the coffee machine on top. An ancient one, had to be years old, the glass jug cloudy from so much use.

"Please. I need something," Kane said, "and don't suggest a drink-drink. I've had enough of alcohol today."

Winter turned his head and raised his eyebrows. "That's got to mean something else. No way would you be drinking on the job."

"No, but someone is."

"Ah."

Winter poured two coffees. Kane's muscles stiffened, and insecurity strangled him in the awkward silence, the lump in his throat painful. Now he'd said something, even if he hadn't named the drinker, he wasn't sure he had the balls to dob Richard in.

Think about what he's been like lately.

Yeah, Richard was a liability, no question, and if Kane wanted to work to the best of his ability, he couldn't carry his partner any longer.

"Tell me," Winter said, placing their cups on the desk, "it's Richard, isn't it?"

Kane hesitated for too long.

"I thought so." Winter sat. Picked up a pen and tapped it on his keyboard. "I've refrained from saying anything, doing anything about it because…" He sighed. "But I'm going to have to do something now. I can see you're worn out by it—that or ready to go a few rounds with him, minus boxing gloves. Hell on the knuckles, that." He smiled. Dropped the pen. Lifted his cup. "Wouldn't advise going down that route." He blew his coffee then sipped. "Can't beat an old-style coffee machine, can you. Stews it better than Granny stews apples."

Kane didn't know what the hell that meant, but he smiled anyway. Tightly. "I don't like grassing on anyone, but Richard—"

"I know. Leave it with me. Drink your coffee. Take a breather."

Kane thought it would be odd sitting there not saying anything, but it wasn't. He cleared his mind of everything and concentrated on chilling out for the time it took to finish his drink.

"Better?" Winter asked.

"Better."

"Now go and do what you do best. I don't want to see you until tomorrow." Winter drained his cup. "Where is he?"

Kane shook his head. "I have no idea. We had a bit of a set-to in the car. He had a hip flask, open, and had smoked at a scene. I lost it. Said some things I maybe shouldn't. He said he had something going on later, that me going on at him wasn't helping." He shrugged. "No idea what he was on about. I came up here, went to my office. Came back out to talk to the team, and Richard wasn't there."

Winter narrowed his eyes. "I see. Right. Thank you. Oh, and you didn't come in to see me, right?"

"No, sir. If I can just ask something... Just say I was getting a new partner... Can you consider Nada?"

"Any particular reason why you think she'd be a good fit?"

"I can list a few. Dependable, trustworthy, hard worker, empathetic, and she deserves a break in life. She gives so much of herself to everyone around her, so it'd be nice if she had something for herself for once."

"That's enough for me. Consider it done. Catch you tomorrow, Kane."

"Right, sir. Thank you."

Kane left, and instead of feeling lighter, vindicated for what he'd done regarding

Richard, two sacks of guilt smacked down onto his shoulders, outweighing the good he'd done by suggesting Nada as his new partner.

The sacks were heavy, the labels on them saying ARSEHOLE.

FOURTEEN

*D*ear Charlotte,
I so hate writing these bleedin' letters. I know why you insist on it, but... Yes, yes, I realise Jez can use your laptop and read your emails. You can't tell me that's normal for a woman to be worried about her boyfriend nosing at her private business. It would be so much easier to speak

on Messenger, and we could talk in real time instead of just once a week via the post.

I miss you. I'll always miss you. And I'll never forgive him for turning you into this recluse who can't even come to see her own mother. I've said this before, in the early years, remember, but you didn't listen, so I kept my mouth shut. But now? Now you've told me he's hitting you and messing about with other women? No more holding my tongue, my girl. It's time to come home.

Ah, don't think I can't see you shaking your head, muttering about him finding you, knowing this is the first place you'll go, but let me tell you something. I know more about Jez than you think, and that man is into some seriously bad business if the rumours are right. Want to know why he keeps you indoors? Why he's restricted Facebook and the like on your laptop and phone? Why he's made it so you can only ring him or businesses, no residential or mobile numbers, like he's got some sort of block going on there? Because he doesn't want you finding out what he's up to. If you can't speak to anyone except that fella over the road, or the old woman you mentioned, you can't gather any evidence.

I'll tell you why he does those things. He deals drugs, Char.

DRUGS. I even underlined, look, because it's a big bloody deal. He supplies to the whole town, and do you know what? I'm going to the police. I have some information that'll put him away, and I'm not afraid to use it. It'll all be set in motion by the time you get this. No going back.

Someone I know, her son gets drugs off him, and Jez, your precious bastard boyfriend, beat the shit out of him because he didn't pay him on time — he'd had some weed on loan a week back. Five minutes late with the payment, he was, and the result? Broken jaw, ribs, leg, and the poor lad was all for telling his mum to keep her mouth shut. She won't. I won't either. I can't bear the thought of you living with a man like that, and what if he drags you into it? Says you're in on it? What if there are drugs in your house, for Pete's sake?

Get out. Come to me, and we'll work something out. Or use that money you told me you've been saving. LEAVE. Go down south, as far as you can go. Cornwall, that'll do. Can't get much farther in the country than the tip of it, can you?

It'll be all right, I promise. Leave everything behind. Don't even pack a bag. Your life is more important than possessions, and from what I've heard, he's got something bigger going on — bigger than before. If he messes with the people he's going to be supplying to, they'll do more than break a few bones. I hope they do. The world's better off shot of him. Good riddance to bad rubbish, I say.

Now, I've said my piece. Take it or leave it, but if you decide to stay, know that I'll love you forever, no matter your decision. I just wish I could make you a pie filled with sense, and when you eat it, you'll truly see the light.

God love you, my darlin'.
Mum

Tears streamed. Charlotte had read the letter three times now, and it hadn't got easier with repetition. She'd been secluded for so long she hadn't a clue who she'd been living with, despite finding those bloody scales and baggies under the sink, and somehow, because her mum had told her things, it seemed a hundred times worse. Why hadn't she listened to her at the beginning? Because she'd thought she knew best, that's why. She'd thought she was in love and that Jez loved her back. But he hadn't. He'd just wanted someone to own, anyone would do, and she'd been the stupid bint who'd fallen for his charms — and he'd had some back then, all sweetness and light, butter wouldn't melt.

God, she'd fallen for it, right down to the bottom of the well.

No more. She knew for sure about him now, and there was no denying it when a copper told you what was going on, too. Now Mum knew, and no wonder people never shopped him to the police if he was going around breaking people's bones.

What kind of monster *was* he?

She had the answer to that already. He'd smacked her around often enough, and she had a few scars to prove it. A hairline one above her lip, and a jagged streak from where he'd shoved her backwards and she'd caught the nape of her neck on the corner of the kitchen island. It had dug in then ripped as she'd gone down, pain searing, blood dripping in a hot stripe down her skin, curving at her shoulder to meander south to pool at the dip above her clavicle.

She should have left then, but he'd locked her in from the outside for a week straight — no idea where he'd stayed — and she'd patched herself up the best she could, and with no sutures to stitch the wound together, it was unsightly, the scar wide.

Charlotte had stopped putting her hair in a ponytail after that.

To take her mind off the past, she moved to the kitchen, shoving things aside in the freezer to find ingredients to make a nice meal for Kane. She'd had enough practise at cooking, one of the main things she'd done at home.

It. Isn't. Home.

While she shallow fried some chicken to seal it, she thought about how, as a kid, she'd loved looking through her mum's recipe book, flour or the odd grain of sugar in the spine side between pages, butter smears in the corners, the scent of cake mixture wafting up. Those days were long gone, light years away, almost as though she hadn't really lived them.

Nostalgia unfurled inside her.

Should she use Kane's house phone to ring her mum? The number was the same as it always was, so Mum had said in a letter once, and it would be lovely to hear her voice again. She hadn't spoken to her since she'd moved into Jez's, not wanting her mother to deal with any backlash—he'd threatened to go round there and 'duff her up', taking Charlotte with him so she could watch.

But what if her mum told her friend Charlotte had called, then that friend told someone else, and eventually, Jez would find out and pay her mum a visit?

No. Charlotte would have to wait until Jez had been put inside.

Then she could talk to her mum as much as she wanted.

FIFTEEN

Kane had a mate who worked at a private lab where, for a price, he'd rush through samples—and rush was the right word. Four hours. Couldn't argue with that, even though he knew damn well testing blood for type only took five minutes. He'd taken the risk earlier and bagged one of the flecks from Pickins' temple and asked a uniform to drop it, and an envelope of money, to Ian Yates, who promised to have it done by one at the latest, but it was past that now. The copper Kane had entrusted it to had agreed to Kane buying him a drink at the local when they were both in there next. Some would say he and Kane were crooked, but he'd argue with that. He did what had to be done, and if it meant spending his own money, getting told off by Winter for breaking rules, so be it.

The rest of the fleck sample, an inside cheek swab from Pickins, the scrapings from beneath his fingernails, and Mrs Smithson's toothbrush had been sent to the usual lab, and the results from that would take between seventy-two hours and four weeks. Six weeks was more likely. Kane didn't have time for that. Now, if the killer turned out to be Pickins, he'd have to wait for the official report to save any inadmissible evidence issues — and the bloke would go free for now anyway until proof had been obtained.

Kane sat at his desk and fired up his computer, accessing his personal email account. Ian had written, the subject line: HERE'S THAT THING YOU ASKED ME TO DO, YOU SHITBAG.

Kane smiled and clicked OPEN.

Fuck.

The blood was the same type as Pickins'.

Shit, shit, shit!

Kane signed out of his account then set the computer to sleep. He still hadn't checked in on Charlotte, but that would have to wait. Kane had a man to release.

Annoyed that the blood was a match to Jez's and not one of the other types, he descended the three flights down to the front desk and drummed his fingertips on top while Vic dealt with some prat who'd been brought in for shoplifting, denying it while the spoils of his adventure sat on the desk inside evidence bags.

Impatient, Kane bit his lip and made eye contact with Vic, who leant over so Kane could speak to him. "Pickins will be leaving shortly, soon as you're ready. I'll just go and inform him now."

Vic nodded and returned to his duties.

Kane took his time on his way to the cells. Four in a row, there were, and he scanned the chalked names on the small board beside each door. Pickins was in the last one. Kane slid open the hatch. Reclined on the bed, Pickins turned his head to look at him.

"Nice nap, that was," he said, sitting up and swinging his legs round, planting his feet on the floor. "So, come to have another pop, have you?"

"You'll be processed shortly," Kane said, voice strained. "You're leaving."

A smug grin appeared. "Good. What's the time?"

Kane checked the clock on the wall above door number three. "Two-forty. Got a hot date?"

"Something like that."

What's he up to? "Don't behave yourself, will you. It'll give me the chance to catch you doing something." Kane slammed the hatch shut, anger beating along with his pulse, fuelling him to kick the wall and curse at the pain lancing up his big toe.

Jez hurried out of the station, hands shoved in his pockets, and scanned Jude Street. Codename H1 (Holder One), the main bloke who stored Jez's drugs, waited in a car a few metres down the way, and Jez got in.

"Cheers, mate," Jez said, clicking his seat belt on. "I would have walked back, but the lousy bastards didn't let me out in time."

"Don't worry about it. There are other things to concern you." H1 peeled away from the kerb. "Your missus was spotted today."

"I see." Jez gritted his teeth. "So much for being taken to a safe house then."

"What?" H1 gripped the steering wheel tight. "We haven't had a chance to talk, have we, so I'm not up to date. Tell me what's going on."

Jez told him about coming home to find Barnett taking Charlotte off, Jez being hauled down the nick because of a few scratches, and, "*My* blood type on my face, no one else's, as I knew it would be. I'd washed the other lot off. Scratch on my face had bled, see, and had dried. I must admit, I thought they had me for a minute there."

H1 nodded. "Glad you're out. Didn't like the idea of all the gear being at mine when it's been promised to the buyer, and you in the nick. Fucked if I'm dealing with the sale — my thought while you were banged up."

"I'm close to the wire, but we should make it. Yeah, we're golden."

"Better be." H1 slowed to a stop outside Jez's gaff. "I'll wait here for you. No point in me coming in. Make it quick, because I have other shit to do. Just a shower you're having, is it?" He pointed to the dash clock. Three-thirty. "Cutting it fine. If you're late…"

"I know." Jez's arsehole spasmed. Last thing he needed was this deal to go belly up. Too much cash depended on it — and his reputation. "The buyer might be a young lad, acts like his antenna doesn't pick up all the channels, but he's clever underneath. It's just a front. I need to be there bang on four, otherwise…"

"Yeah, *otherwise* isn't a good option, because if you mess this up, you'll be viewed as someone who eats soup with a fork, know what I mean?"

"Ha ha. Yeah." Jez would normally have flattened someone for saying that, but H1 had been his informant for years, someone he trusted, who had his back. Jez could take a jibe or two off him without having to retaliate. He opened the door. "Right, give me five."

He went in the house, frowning at the chill in the hallway. A draught coasted towards him, and he moved into the kitchen. The back door stood open a crack. He'd shut it last night, hadn't he? Jez had had a quick ciggie in the garden after Charlotte and Barnett had left, and he was sure he'd locked it — or at least closed it — when that other copper had knocked to take him to the station.

He secured it then did a sweep of the house — nothing out of place or missing. Had someone broken in thinking he kept his stash at his own digs? If they had, they'd been tidy about it — and sorely mistaken.

With no time to think about it, he showered, threw some clothes on, and got back in H1's car.

"All set?" H1 asked.

"Yeah."

They arrived at the meeting spot, a street of decrepit houses that reminded Jez of his roots. He hated it around here, all those memories, the only bright one in it his sister. He loved her still, even all these years after her death. Everything he did was in her honour, although she'd be devastated to have learned what he did for a living.

He'd been building himself up to be top dog, and although he was, this new fella on the scene, today's buyer…there was something about him Jez didn't like.

He itched to take him down a peg.

Jez could supply whatever the young lad wanted, and as long as the kid didn't pull rank, everything would bob along just fine. But if he *did* try to take over… Jez wasn't sure he was hard enough to take him on. Although Jez was a beefcake, he'd heard his buyer was into some of that judo shit or other martial arts where you said "Yah!" every time you hand-chopped someone. One well-placed kick, and your nuts slid up into your throat, that kind of thing.

Coaching himself on remaining calm and hopefully giving off the aura he wasn't to be messed with, Jez got out of the car and strode up the path of number seventy-two. An old fridge had its arse parked in front of a gate next to the house, the door open, revealing mould on the shelves and bits of dried cheese even a mouse would turn its nose up at. A black refuse sack, bulging, yellow tie handles trembling in the breeze, had holes the sides.

Damn cats.

He sniffed — hadn't had any coke for a while; might treat himself to some when he got home — and knocked on the door. The buyer opened it. A slim line of rooftop-shaped hair lived under his nose, plucked by the look of it, resembling the one What's His Face had, that bloke in the black-and-white films. Name like a shoe shop. Clark? His black hair was slicked back the same and all, and his suit appeared out of place in that house — rich versus poor.

"Show me," Jez said, oozing authority, rolling his shoulders and puffing his chest out.

The buyer kicked a holdall closer to the door, the front of his wingtip shoe disappearing into a fold of material. Wasn't the bag full then? He partially unzipped it. Bundles of cash, that's what Jez liked to find, and it reached the top.

"Now *you* show *me*," the lad said.

Jez wanted to throw some rebuke at him but didn't at the last minute. He liked his teeth the way they were, thank you. Back at the car, he tapped on H1's tinted window. A sharp click, then the boot slowly lifted. He hefted out two of his own holdalls — a tenner each, Sports Direct online, got a free mug the size of a skyscraper with the order — and carried them up the path to the front door. The buyer must have people hidden, keeping an eye out, because Jez sensed he was being watched.

He drew the zip across on each bag, a quarter of the way along, the product green, quality shag in one, the other white and cut with things that shouldn't be too taxing on the internal organs.

The buyer nodded. "Exchange." He reached out and took the powder bag.

At the same time, Jez grabbed for the cash. Money held in front of him, Jez waited while his customer collected the second bag. "Let me know if you want any more."

"Can you get the same to me by this time next week?"

Jez nodded. "Crops are doing well all over town—great strain this time round, growing like weeds." He laughed, hale and hearty.

The buyer didn't.

Jez cleared his throat. How could someone so young unnerve a man like him? *Fucking little cock*. "And I'm due another batch of the other stuff in two days, so yeah."

"Make sure you deliver it on time."

Jez's heart skipped a beat. "I'm on time today."

"Heard you might not have been. Best you don't get yourself banged up again."

"Or what?" The words were out before he'd had a chance to stop them.

"Or I'll slit your throat."

The way he'd said that… Chills broke out all over Jez's body, and he laughed to cover up his immense discomfort. "Whatever, mate."

"I'm not your mate."

This bloke didn't seem right in the head, one twist short of a Slinky, and for the first time in his life, Jez wanted to back away from someone. The buyer's eyes had a maniacal gleam, at odds with his passive expression. Blank, he looked, as though he hadn't just threatened to kill Jez.

"Shame we're not mates," Jez said, "because I'm good to have on your side."

Jez turned and stalked down the path, and whoever had been observing the exchange was still there, holed up somewhere, the force of their stares seeming to burn into him. He closed the boot he'd left wide open then got in the passenger seat, dumping the holdall on his lap. H1 sped off, and Jez waited until they were well away before he pulled three bundles out and tossed them in his footwell.

"Three?" H1 frowned.

"Call it a bonus."

"Thanks."

It was actually to keep H1 sweet in case that old-fashioned-looking twat back there started any funny business. H1 was a mean bastard when he wanted to be. A great ally who didn't mind getting blood on his hands.

Kane stared at the whiteboard and the timeline written out for the Smithson murder. Every neighbour appeared accounted for except for Pickins. His alibi of being in bed with Charlotte was false, and although Kane could say he'd seen her in the pub, he hadn't wanted to tell Pickins where she'd really been. If Charlotte didn't leave town and start afresh elsewhere, she still risked seeing Pickins, and Kane wouldn't put it past the man to give her a clip round the earhole, even if they were no longer a couple.

His office phone rang, and he went in there to answer it.

"Vic, sir."

"Got something for me?"

"You have a visitor. She's in the waiting room. Rothers, her name is."

What the hell is Charlotte doing here? "I'll be down in a second. Thanks."

He barrelled out of his office, through the incident room, and at the front desk, eyed the civilians sitting there. None of them were Charlotte.

"Where is she?" he said to Vic.

"Just there, sir. Animal coat."

There she was, a woman, about fifty-five, leopard-print leggings, furry light-brown jacket, over-the-knee black boots, Bet Lynch from *Corrie* on acid, complete with bottle-blonde beehive.

What the actual?

She stood, minced over to him, and tilted her head sharply towards the door on Kane's right which led to interview rooms. Blue makeup shadowed the lids of her bright-green eyes, kohl thickly drawn below with a not-quite-steady hand. Skin like a goddamned walnut shell. Red lipstick bled onto the outer skin in thinner-than-hair spiderwebs, a chunk of it gathering in one corner. She smiled, revealing lipstick on her teeth, too.

Bloody hell…

"Quickly," she said. "Before someone comes in who I know."

Kane glanced at Vic, who pressed a flat red button on the wall, and the door buzzed. Kane pushed it open, and Mrs Rothers scuttled through, spindly legs so thin he wondered how they held her up.

The light above interview room four was on. "Room one," he said and plugged a code into the metal panel on the wall beside the jamb. He

141

allowed her to go in first. "Please, sit down, won't you?"

She perched on a plastic black chair, its legs scuffed, silver showing through where the coating had been scratched over the years.

"What can I do for you, Mrs Rothers?" he asked and sat opposite on the other side of the desk.

She produced a phone from her bag—big enough to carry twin babies in—and jabbed at the screen a few times. "I think you'll want to see this."

She handed him the phone.

Kane looked at the image.

And smiled.

"You'll need to set up a meeting with that man in the suit," she said. "He's not available for a week, though, but rest assured, the stuff in the two bags he took from Jez isn't going anywhere. Another exchange has been organised for the same time next week, four o'clock, and him there"—she pointed at the suited fella—"wants you at that house while it goes on."

"Why has he done this?" Kane asked. "Not that I'm complaining, mind. We need all the help we can get."

"Well, that Jez busted his brother up something bad—broken this and that—and he wanted to get him back for it. Thought the best way was to pose as a buyer, get Jez's trust with the first drop-off, so he'd come back the following week. The money he paid is fake. High-quality, you'd never know the difference apparently. Amazing how quick these counterfeit people can copy the new versions of notes. And you'll forgive me for not telling you their names. They've helped out, see."

Kane thought of that money getting lost amongst the real stuff and winced.

"Oh, don't you go looking like that," she said. "Cos you'll want to have a peek at this and all." She drew a piece of laminated A4 out of her bag and pushed it across the table. "Serial numbers for all the notes. You alert all the banks or whatever you do in these situations." She smiled, her teeth the kind you put in a glass of water at night. "I'll be off, then. Got a back way I can nip through, have you?"

Kane nodded. "If you don't mind me asking…why are you doing this?"

"For my daughter," she said.

"Charlotte?"

Her mouth gaped.

"Thought so." He rested a hand on her shoulder. "She's safe, you know. Not with him anymore."

"Shut the front door!"

He laughed at the expression. "She's fine. Just give her a few days—or until after the second exchange—and I'm sure she'll come to see you."

Tears filled her eyes. "Gawd…" She sniffed. "That man will be in contact soon. The exchanger, I mean."

"Thank you," he said. "I'll never forget this, I promise you. I've been after Pickins for years."

"You and me both."

SIXTEEN

Debbie shovelled a forkful of Bolognese sauce into her mouth and burnt her tongue. Well, *that* was going to spoil their first kiss later, wasn't it. She silently cursed Mum for making the dinner too hot and ruining what could have been something wonderful if her taste buds weren't throbbing.

"What's the rush, Deb?" Dad asked.

"Got homework to do, then I'm meeting the gang at the park. Be back about ten, yeah?"

"Make sure you get that lad Ben to walk you home." Dad twirled spaghetti. "Aren't you two an item yet?"

Keeping up the façade—she'd told them she fancied Ben to get them off the scent of who she really had her eye on—she said, "Not yet, but I'm hoping he says he'll go out with me tonight."

"Nice boy," Mum said, "although his mother's a bit of a snooty one. So glad I don't have to walk you to school anymore. She used to look down her nose at me in the playground."

"She might be part of the family one day," Dad said. "So be careful what you say to our Debbie."

Debbie tuned them out, thinking of her fantasy guy and what they'd get up to once she was on the other side of his front door. With her alibi etched in stone, she could enjoy herself without worrying.

Must remember to set an alarm on my phone so I'm not home late.

After dinner, she helped load the dishwasher, taking her time so it meant wasting more. It was quarter to six now—still so long to wait—so she offered to make her parents a cuppa.

"What are you after?" Mum asked, smiling.

"Nothing!" Debbie flushed. "Can't I make you tea now?"

"Oh, you're welcome to make it all right, but you've never done it before, so I'm wondering if you even know how." Mum ruffled her hair.

Totally bugging.

"I won't bother then," Debbie said and flounced off up the stairs.

Why did they have to say stuff like that?

She sat on her bed and stroked the outfit she'd chosen. A lovely red dress. Fake black leather jacket. And Converses, black with white trim. She reckoned he'd like her in those.

She texted her friends to let them know she couldn't come out because she had a boyfriend now and was busy this evening. A flurry of responses came back.

WHO IS IT?
DO WE KNOW HIM?
WHAT ABOUT BEN?

She sighed. What about him? He was childish.

She didn't reply. They wouldn't understand, anyway, so what was the point?

Huffing out a breath to calm the rapid butterfly wings in her belly, she ran a bath, humming Ed Sheeran's *Perfect* and imagining her fantasy guy singing it to her. It could be their song, and they'd dance to it at their wedding, and later, every time it came on the radio, they'd smile that secret smile of love and gaze at each other until the last note ended.

In the bath, she shaved her legs, armpits, and down below — not that she had much hair there anyway. She'd heard some men liked women without any, so she went the whole hog and lopped the lot off.

Finished and in her room, she checked the time — OMG, she'd been in the bath so long; seven o'clock — then quickly gave her hair a blow-dry, putting it up in a messy bun. She looked older that way, so that was sick, fam. She cringed at falling into the way her friends spoke. She had to stop that if she wanted to come off as mature, would do anything to appear as though she could be his girlfriend without people frowning at the age gap. They'd get through anything together, though, wouldn't they? Love was strong like that.

She applied foundation and eyeshadow, stuck on fake eyelashes, and concentrated on using the kohl pencil, singing their song and tearing up at the line about her looking perfect tonight. Her eyeliner wing smudged, and it took a fair bit of repair work until she was satisfied with it. Her face didn't seem like hers now. She was eighteen, twenty maybe. Shame she was still almost sixteen inside, those butterflies misbehaving again.

Not long to go now, and she'd be in his arms.

If she sang their song through twelve more times, she reckoned it would just about be five to eight.

SEVENTEEN

Sitting on the dining room chair, Charlotte gasped at the sound of a key in the door, for a moment forgetting where she was, thinking she was back at home and Jez was coming in. She caught sight of the baking tray she'd cooked the enchiladas in, sitting on top of the shiny, ultra-modern stove, and remembered she was safe, that it was just Kane, no one else.

He appeared in the kitchen doorway, blinked while staring at the dinner, then switched his attention to her. His smile lit up everything inside her, and she tamped down the happiness—it was too dangerous to like him, to want to be with him, to think he'd even want a fucked-up woman like her. Besides, how could she trust another man again, copper or not, after what Jez had done to her? Her mum had been lucky with Charlotte's dad, but they hadn't had much time together before—

"You cooked." Kane walked over to the large bowls she'd set out on the work surface—salad, home-baked soda bread because he had no yeast in the cupboard. He lifted the tea towels covering them. "You actually *made* that bread?"

"Well, yes." What was so amazing about that? "You said not to leave the house, so I couldn't buy any. What you had in the crock over there was mouldy, so I put it in the bin."

I wish I didn't have to lie about not leaving the house. He's been good to me. I should tell him…

He shook his head. "Jez has no idea, has he?"

"No idea of what?" She felt sick.

"No idea what he had in you."

To mask her surprise at his compliment, if that's what it was, she jumped up to dish some enchiladas onto a plate then warm them up in the microwave. While the three minutes ticked by, she poured wine into bulbous glasses, possibly meant for brandy, but it didn't matter, did it, and all the time he watched her from a seat at the table, the one she'd vacated.

"Been a long time since anyone cooked for me," he said, flicking a fork handle back and forth.

"Been a long time since I cooked for anyone who was interested in the result. Mostly, it ended up in the bin because he'd eaten elsewhere." The microwave dinged, and she pulled out the steaming food, sharing it between two fresh plates.

Once she'd carried everything to the table, pleased Kane hadn't got up to help—she was better left alone in that respect—she sat, and they locked gazes.

Kane looked away first.

Good. It saved her having to do it.

"Eat up then," she said, serving him some salad.

"You don't have to wait on me," he said. "But I appreciate it. Long day. Had a bit of a barny with a colleague, who then went missing for the rest of the shift. Had to do something I've been putting off for a while, too, but never mind about that." He paused, then, spreading butter on a thick slice of bread, said, "I have some news for you."

Her stomach flipped. Would she always be a nervous wreck? Even when speaking with Kane in the pub, then going to the hotel with him, she'd imagined she'd been watched by everyone, Jez's spies as customers, people on the streets, the hotel staff. She had a feeling it would never leave her, this out-of-sorts, anxious discombobulation. She'd just have to learn to live with it, hopefully to a lesser degree.

"What's happened?" she asked, her appetite dying a little, the edge of her hunger shaved away by his six sharp words.

"I saw your mother today."

"*What*?" She scraped her chair back over the white floor tiles, panic sluicing through her, knees weakening until they lost their rigidity and she thought she might fall. What had Jez done? Had he gone round there and hurt her? "What… Is she all right?" Her cheeks heated to an uncomfortable degree, and she flapped her hands in front of her face, fork still held in one. She dropped it onto her plate.

"She's fine, Charlotte. What's the *matter* with you?" He frowned. "Sit down, will you?"

She lowered to her seat, shaking, the fright she'd had covering her skin with shock-induced pimples, the hairs on her arms standing on end. "You…I…I thought…"

"Bloody hell, I didn't think this through very well, did I?" He reached across to hold one of her trembling hands. "I'm sorry. I didn't realise your mind would go *there*."

"Well, it did," she said quietly, hardly hearing herself. "It always does. He can't…you can't let him go near my mum."

"He didn't, he won't, I promise. Take a sip of that wine and a second to calm down. Shit. Again, I'm so sorry."

It appeared he wanted to kick himself, and she felt for him, sitting there like that with his face showing how upset he was, his mouth drooping, his eyes heavy-lidded, so she turned her hand over beneath his and curled her fingers to hold him tight.

"I told you," she said. "I told you I knew he'd hurt her if I disobeyed him and ever visited her. I imagined he thought you'd taken me to her place, and he went there to find me, and when I wasn't there he…"

"Hurt her," he finished. "Christ."

She gulped some wine and winced. She'd never been a fan of dry. Hated the way it left her tongue feeling as though she'd sucked on a lemon. "So how did you see her? Did you call on her?"

"No, she came to see me. Eat while I tell you. You've gone white."

"*She* came to see *you*?" She almost dropped her glass.

"Just listen, all right?"

154

She closed her mouth, placing her wine on the coaster, and he told her everything. She recalled a few lines from her mum's letter, and it all made sense now.

I should have expected something like this.

"She...did she have anything to do with the actual 'sting', as you put it?" She pushed out a long breath. One of the napkins she'd folded into a swan earlier keeled over. She likened it to herself, knocked off her feet by his revelation.

"No, but she knew quite a bit about how it went down, so I'm thinking the mother of the lad who'd been beaten and his brother...well, they probably told her what was going on."

"Did she look well?" She thought of the man who'd got into her taxi. How was *his* mother?

"She looked...not what I expected."

Charlotte laughed, knowing exactly what he wasn't saying. Her mum's dress sense was outrageous, mutton dressed as lamb some would say, but she had a heart of gold to go with her sometimes potty mouth, and Charlotte had missed her so, so much. "She's...flamboyant, hmm? What was she wearing?" She smiled, waiting for his answer.

"You ever heard of Bet Lynch?"

She nodded.

"That." He grinned. "Leopard print, as I recall. Fur."

"Mum used to go on about Bet. *Coronation Street*, I think." God, it was so good to giggle, to feel like she had all those years ago, before her life had gone down a path tangled with poisonous weeds instead of flowers.

"You don't resemble her."

"No, I look like my dad." She sobered, laughter disappearing as though it had been corked inside a bottle.

"You don't see him either?" He cut into his so-far-untouched enchilada, popping some into his mouth.

"Never met him." And it didn't hurt that she hadn't, not really, although she'd have loved to have seen him just once in the flesh instead of on an old, faded photograph that had been touched so many times by her mum over the years that the surface reminded her of snakeskin, the corners curled. The area over her father's face was worn from her mum stroking it so much, the gloss of the image turning matt. God only knew what state it was in now. Maybe his face had gone altogether. If it had, did her mum remember what he'd looked like, or had his features faded without the visual reminder like they had for Charlotte? "He, uh, he died before I was born. Fell fifty feet off some scaffolding. Hit the ground. He didn't die right away... A few hours later."

"Blimey, I'm sorry."

She shrugged. "How's your dinner?"

"I wanted to tell you, it's sodding gorgeous, but there wasn't an appropriate time. Thank you" — he pointed his fork at his plate — "for doing this. You didn't have to."

"I did. I'm camping out in your house. It's fine. You're helping me, so it's the least I can do." She tucked into her food, hungry again.

The meal went by without them speaking, and once they were done, she automatically rose to clear the plates away.

"This is where I put my foot down," he said. "You cooked, I clean." He pointed to her chair. "Sit."

She obeyed instantly, what he'd said alien to her — why would he want to clean? — and his eyes widened, a flush creeping into his cheeks.

"Shit." He pulled at his hair. "I didn't like what just happened there."

"What are you on about?" She frowned.

"I said sit, and you did it immediately, quickly, like you were scared."

Had she? "Oh."

"You should find someone to speak to when this is all over. You know, to get some things off your chest. To understand that not everyone expects you to behave a certain way like Pickins did." He placed her plate on top of his. "I'd have suggested a Dr George Schumer in the next city over, but, uh, he was killed so…" He shrugged. "Maybe you can find someone yourself, eh?"

"Maybe."

Kane smiled, and while he cleared things away, she stared out into the garden, at the tree silhouettes, the tops kale-like against a strange, orange-grey sky, the kind before night fully forces its way in to allow the stars to shine.

"This time next week it'll all be over," he said, dropping the cutlery into the dishwasher basket so the blades and fork tines jutted upwards. "Think you can stand that long holed up in here?"

"I've done it for sixteen years, so…" She drank some more wine, her mouth in need of fluid. It was gross but better than nothing.

"Then you can move on." He finished stacking plates in the machine, dropped a cleaning tablet into the bottom, and set the wash to start.

The hum of the machine was exactly the same as hers, except it wasn't hers anymore, and she'd rather do the dishes by hand than ever go back there and use it again. "I can't believe it's happening. That I got away." A sense of bewilderment filled her, and she struggled with the emotions running riot.

"I'm glad you decided to go out last night. It was…it was great," he said. Was he blushing?

"I, um, I hadn't been with anyone for a while until you came along."

This was getting too personal. Last night she'd wanted revenge sex, and she'd had it, with his assurance they wouldn't do it again, but after, he'd wanted more, and now it seemed he wanted to talk about things they shouldn't. "Stop it."

He washed his hands and dried them on a tea towel. "Yeah. I should, shouldn't I. And I will. Want to watch TV?"

"Okay." She didn't—didn't want to do anything really except sit where she was and imagine her mum in her whacky clothes. But she followed him into the living room, taking the wine she didn't want either.

She was used to doing things she had no desire to do.

EIGHTEEN

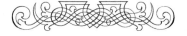

She turned up about half an hour ago, a couple of minutes early, but that's all right, though if she doesn't do exactly as she's told *next* time, I'm liable to get arsey.

That happens a lot.

She's dressed like a slut—like those prossers from last night. Tarty. Asking for it. Come and take my knickers off and show me your cock.

Where's the class gone these days? Why do most women wear stuff that makes them appear cheap? Gets right on my nerves. Then again, I'm a walking contradiction. I use those types of women, I *go* with the ragbags, maybe because it gives me a sense of superiority.

Who the fuck knows.

She's eaten the Belgian bun, and the can of Coke is on the coffee table, don't think she's drunk much of it. I'd offer her the other type of coke, but it'd be wasted on her. She's sitting on my sofa beside me, knees together, her legs smooth, but there's a speck of blood on one of them. Probably where she nicked it shaving. Novice at the job, not enough practice to know you can slice your skin off with one of those razors if you're not careful.

Silly cow.

She's humming some tune or other, and it's winding me up because I've heard it before and can't place it, but I won't show I'm peeved.

Not just yet.

"That's a nice tune," I say, lying through my sodding teeth.

"It's Ed," she says.

I know exactly what song it is now, remembering the words, and I could just smash her face in at her naivety, at how she thinks her being here is something it's not. Oh, he loves me. He thinks I'm the best.

The mantelpiece catches my attention, the town crier's bell a wicked taunt, and I grind my teeth. It'd make a good weapon, that, if I could bear to touch it, to smack it onto her air-filled head, but it would ring, and then I wouldn't be able to go through with my plans.

"How's school?" I ask.

She raises her shoulders. "Oh, it's all right. I feel too old to be there, know what I mean? Can't wait to leave. Got another two years, though, now they've made it so you have to stay until you're eighteen. I hate that rule."

I've got a few rules I need you to learn, and one of them is to stop pissing me off.

"Don't you like your lessons then?" I smile.

It's tight.

She smiles back. Coy. Making out she's shy. "Some are okay. Have *you* got anything to teach me?"

Dear oh Lord.

"I do as it happens, but my classroom's at the end of the garden."

Wink.

She perks up, all ears. "What's down there then?"

Like I said, my classroom.

Why don't they listen?

"Oh, I've got a brick summer house. Nice. It's got electricity, basically a room, except it isn't connected to the house. Soundproofed, too."

"Oh, d'you play loud music in there or something?"

Or something.

"Want to see?" I stand and hold my hand out to her.

She grabs it, palms clammy, maybe she's nervous, and it turns me the hell off. Like sucking her hair did. She licks her lips, bats her eyelids; really does have the makings of becoming a slapper, this one.

"Is it dark in there?" she asks. "Because I like *doing it* with the lights on."

This is just getting worse.

"I like to see everything," she says.

If I were a better person, I'd feel sorry for her. But I'm not. So I don't. Seduction is not her forte. She's trying too hard, and I wonder why I ever thought I could have her in my life in *that* way.

"Handy that there's no windows out there then, so people can't see us getting it on." I laugh at myself.

"This is really happening," she breathes, her face showing her age, the kid she is. It's like she's an eight-year-old on her birthday.

I don't answer, just give her a grin, and she seems okay with that.

I lead her through the hallway, the kitchen, then out onto the path made of round flagstones set a footstep apart in a curve. We reach the line of tall trees in front of my 'den', and I pull her between two and open the door an inch or so, the darkness within a long stripe against the white jamb.

"Close your eyes before I turn the light on," I whisper, checking the backs of the adjacent houses to make sure no one's at their window. The police have gone, so I haven't got to worry about any of them turning up.

"Okay," she says then giggles — too loudly.

"*Shh*," I say. "You don't want anyone recognising that sexy laugh of yours and telling your mum and dad where you are, do you?"

"Sorry."

You will be.

I hold my hand over her eyes, her lashes flickering on my palm — she hasn't done as she's told, damn it. I resist lowering my hand over her nose and mouth like I did to that bird last night. I have to get her inside.

I nudge her arse with my knee, and she enters, hands out in front of her, as though she's about to pin the tail on the motherfucking donkey. I shut the door so it's pitch black and feel for the metal panel that will cover the door and suction-lock to the metal wall once I press the remote to make it slide across.

The sound of the soft *schlup* when it connects is almost as orgasmic as her panicked breathing.

"Keep your eyes closed for just a minute longer, then you can see my classroom."

"You *are* funny," she says, her voice riddled with a tremble. "Before you show me, though, can I just ask you something?"

She's ruining the big reveal.

"All right." I sigh quietly.

"What's the deal with Charlotte?"

Oh. She's said the wrong thing.

Silly, silly girl.

NINETEEN

Debbie was so excited she could barely stand it. The tension mounted in the darkness, and seeing was like trying to stop Brexit, no way, no how. Until the light came on, she was stuck in a black void that had her thinking she'd been transported somewhere else — purgatory, that in-between place you went before you moved on to Heaven or Hell. The thought unnerved her, and for a tiny speck of time, she asked herself if it had been a mistake to come here.

He was a man, she was a girl. A big difference.

Then her ego trounced in, all big mouth and look-at-me-I'm-a-know-it-all — hey, you're a teenager, so there you go — and she knew she could handle whatever went on in his summer house. She should feel privileged to be here and betted he didn't bring just anyone into his private space.

She was special.

"Where are you?" she asked.

"*Shh* a minute. I'm busy."

Doing what?

Something smelt funny. She sniffed, picking up his scent plus another, one she couldn't work out. Then a memory kicked in. It was kind of like the smell of a Barbie's hair or her Girl's World's when it had been new and fresh out of the box.

"Right!"

She jumped at his voice, so soft, breathy, more like he'd said *riiiiight* in the way Dad did when he sighed the word after something disappointing had happened.

"Before the light goes on, I've got a game to play."

Why was he talking like that? Like a...like a woman?

"It's my version of Guess Who, except it's called Guess What."

He sounded so close, yet she couldn't sense him anywhere near. An invisible cloud enveloped her, a sense of menace and uncertainty seeping off it and into her, unsettling her so much that for a moment she wanted to blurt—

I need to go home. Please, let me go home.

So much for thinking she could handle this.

She didn't say anything, though. If she did, she wouldn't have him for a boyfriend then a husband, because he'd know she wasn't mature enough, and her whole life would turn out differently to what she'd planned. This had been almost three years in the making—two and three-quarter years of pining, hoping, setting everything in motion. It'd be such a shame and a waste if she gave in at the first hurdle. It was the dark doing this to her, that was all, and he'd only sounded weird because her mind was playing tricks on her.

"Okay," she managed, her voice as breathy as his.

"Over here then."

His hand curled around her wrist, and she shrank back, startled.

It's only him. It's okay.

He tugged her, and she stepped forward, and it was weird that even though she knew it was just a room, she didn't trust her footing. There could be anything in here — furniture in the way or whatever — and it was all right for him, he knew the layout, so he'd navigate without a problem.

"Just here," he said.

"You don't sound right." It popped out, and she cursed herself. She should have kept her mouth shut.

"It doesn't matter what I sound like." It was him again, his voice this time, angry, impatient. "Don't talk now unless I tell you to or ask you a question."

She had the fleeting thought that someone else was in there with them, and a shudder raced through her. "Okay."

"What did I just say?"

She stayed mute.

"I *said*: Don't talk unless I tell you to or ask you a question." He squeezed her wrist and gave it a bit of a shake.

Pins and needles in her palm, she swallowed, her throat tight, tears threatening. Why was he so angry? Why was he being like this? He'd never struck her as the mardy type before, so why was he like it now? She blinked to stop her eyes leaking, but they did anyway, hot liquid sliding down her cheeks, cold by the time it reached her jaw.

"Now," he said, sounding female again and lifting her hand. "You need to guess what you're touching. You have three guesses. One, two, three!"

She opened her mouth to say she had to go home then remembered he'd told her not to speak. Instead, she held her breath and pressed her lips together.

He lowered her hand, and her fingertips came into contact with whatever it was she had to guess at.

"Feel it," he said, high-pitched.

She moved her finger. The item was small, marble-sized, rounded on one end, kind of straight on the other. The curved end was smooth, but the straight was bumpy, reminding her of an uneven scab.

"I'll turn it over," he said. "Now touch it again."

The other side was hard, and she tried to wrench her hand away, but he held her wrist steady, and she lost the battle of strength.

"It's time to guess, Debbie. Speak."

She didn't have a clue. "A pebble?"

"Wrong." His voice.

"Um…a piece of food?"

"Wrooooong." The other voice.

"I…I don't know."

"*Think!*" His voice.

Scared now, she fought against his hold, but he seemed intent on keeping her hand above the thing she'd touched. His nails dug into the underside of her wrist, painful and sharp.

Just guess anything so this will stop.

"A dried-up meatball." Stupid answer, but it had been the first thing to come to mind.

"Wrong. Again." The other voice.

Confused as to why another person was in here—because there had to be, no way he could sound like that—she pouted at the unfairness of this. What was going on? Her plan had been ruined by this stupid game, and her future seemed uncertain, her dreams of them together splintering the longer she stayed there with him. If she could get out, go home, perhaps tomorrow they could start again, and everything would turn out as she'd envisaged.

"I'm going to let you see what you touched," the other person said in that weird, whispery cadence. "Wait a moment."

He let go of her wrist, and she immediately brought it up to her chest to rub it with her other hand. Hot, the skin itched, and she'd swear he'd taken off the top layer. It hurt the same way as when she'd held her arm over the steam coming out of the kettle spout for a dare. See how long you can take the pain. The person with the longest amount of seconds wins.

Something was being moved. The slightest of noises, a scraping so faint she wasn't sure she was even hearing right.

"All my little prizes in a row," the other person said.

What's she on about? And who is she anyway?

That lost feeling came, the one where her mind told her to make sense of this, to find a logical explanation, her heart whispering for Mum, saying sorry for getting annoyed at her when she'd made the joke about the cups of tea. Debbie hadn't called out and said goodbye when she'd left, still too angry to give them the time of day, but now she wished she had, just so she'd heard: *Love you, Deb! Stay safe!*

Love

You

Deb

Stay

Safe…

Was she safe now? She thought she was — overreacting was one of her strong points — but then she thought she wasn't. This wasn't a fun game, this Guess What, and as for there being three of them in his summer house, *that* hadn't been what she'd expected. It was supposed to be only Debbie and him, spending the evening together, Debbie becoming a woman.

"There. Don't you look nice?" the third party said.

Who is she speaking to? Me? And how can she see in the dark?

"You *do* look nice," he said. "So pretty."

Debbie frowned and backed away.

"Where do you think *you're* going?" the woman asked.

"I...I need..."

"Don't speak unless I say you can," he said.

He gripped her wrist again, and God, it hurt, disinfectant on scraped knees, salt and vinegar crisps on an ulcer in your mouth.

"Back over here." He guided her forward.

She tried to resist, to dig her feet right into the floor, but he was strong, and she slid, almost losing her balance.

"Stop being such a child," he said.

"I told you not to bring her," the woman said.

"I had to. She needs the lessons."

Lessons? "I don't want lessons anymore. I want to go home." *I want Mum, Dad, Squiggly.* My God did she want Squiggly, his fur beneath her hands, his bacon tongue lolling when she threw him a stick in the field at the park.

A lump formed in her throat—*it's aching, aching so bad*—and she couldn't swallow it. Panicked, she struggled to breathe, her heart thrumming a wicked beat, super-fast, then *so* slow she counted several seconds between each one.

"Get ready," he said.

173

The woman giggled.

He pushed Debbie's head down so her chin touched something hard, cold. "This is exactly where you need to be."

She closed her eyes. Scrunched them up.

"Don't do that. You need to *see*," he said.

A light had switched on; the insides of her eyelids flared pink. Still she kept her eyes closed, instinct telling her she *didn't* want to see, *shouldn't* see.

"Open. Them." He was angry.

She didn't want him to be angry.

Slowly, she cracked one eye open, just a slit. It took a moment for her mind to register what was in front of her, that the item was so close it almost brushed the ends of her false lashes. She widened both eyes then, blinking, blinking, lashes brushing the tops of her cheeks, and shook her head slightly, thinking: *No. This isn't real.*

The 'in a row' comment came back to her, and she fully accepted that, side by side, four fingertips and a thumb sat on a metal table, the scratches on the stainless steel thin as a wisp and numerous, overlapping, criss-crossed. She yanked her head up, ripped her hand out of his hold, and backed away one step, two steps, bumping into someone behind, struggling not to scream. She stared ahead, to each side and, seeing no one, spun to face whoever blocked her reversal.

She gasped, hand automatically flying to her mouth, her heart threatening to give out, burst, her legs wobbling, nausea swarming into her stomach, a miasmic gas that shot out of her mouth in a great gust, flowing on the wings of terror.

Someone stood there, Dolly Parton hair, so yellow it had to be a wig — *that smell, that was the smell, Barbie…* Steampunk goggles covered the lady's eyes, and Debbie vaguely acknowledged that was how this woman had seen in the dark. And the woman had facial hair, just like his, and it was weird and wrong and frightening and confusing. Debbie cried out, snapping her eyes this way and that in search of the door, but the room had steel walls, no apparent way to exit.

How did we get in then? How am I even here?

The woman lowered the goggles, and they dangled around her neck on a thick black strap. "Do you want to go home, Debbie?" she asked in his voice.

Should she speak? Keep quiet? Survival instinct kicked in. "Yes. Yes. Please, let me go home."

The woman smiled, showing *his* teeth, a row of porcelain, each top arch the same shape as the M logo for McDonald's. "What do you think, sister?" His voice.

"Oh, I don't think so." Her voice. "She needs to go."

Go? Yes, she needed to go. "Please, yes, let me go."

"But you're not going anywhere," the woman said.

Muddled, her mind spinning, Debbie lost it and ran to the left, to where she thought they'd come in. She slapped the wall, screaming, crying for Mum, asking God, her nan in Heaven, for anyone, someone to help her.

Then the vague shape of someone standing in the corner loomed fuzzy in her peripheral, and she glanced at it—someone bald, someone with strange shiny skin—and she screamed so hard her throat hurt.

"Nasty noise, soooo nasty," the woman said in her ear from behind.

A sharp pain jabbed Debbie's shoulder, shutting her up mid-wail, and she turned her head to look at it. A syringe sat there, then a thumb appeared in Debbie's line of vision and pressed the plunger.

For a second or two, Debbie stared, thinking absolutely nothing, shock emptying her head. Then she screamed again, her body numbing, a wave of lethargy swamping her muscles, her bladder emptying, urine slithering down her legs and into her Converses.

Then she slumped to the floor.

TWENTY

She's on the floor in a heap, lying in her own piss. Stupid mare. Filthy tart. She forced me to do that, to shut her up with the syringe. Her voice was too much. My sister didn't like it. Now I'm going to have to wait an hour or two — three, four, I don't bloody know — before I can teach her some lessons. That isn't how I thought things would pan out, but you can't predict everything, can you?

I take my sister's hair off and step to the mannequin in the corner, placing it on the head. Using the brush off the nearby shelf, I groom the strands until they're nice and tidy. I hang my goggles on the mannequin's wrist then contemplate how to spend the time before Debbie wakes.

While I undress the mannequin, I think about the things on the table.

I don't believe Debbie truly appreciated what I was showing her. Ungrateful bitch, typical teenager. It took effort to chop that prosser's fingertips and thumb off, and all Debbie could do was walk backwards as though desperate to get away from them.

Rude.

She's going to be hard work, I can see that now, and I wish I hadn't invited her here to my special place. It's too late to send her home; this has gone too far for that, and she's seen too much. That's an inconvenience, but nothing I can't fix.

I bundle the mannequin's clothes up and pop them into a drawer of a filing cabinet beside my desk. Then I take out the syringe, toss it away, and peel Debbie's jacket off her, the trashy, supposedly sexy red dress that is anything but, and the wet shoes. I stare at her underwear, at

179

the black knickers with a red ribbon bow at the side, and the black bra, a red rose between the cups. I remove them, and as I turn to carry the clothing to the mannequin, something drops to the floor with a dull *thwack*.

What the fuck *is* that?

I crouch, pick it up, hold it in my palm. It's one of those chicken fillet things, the kind women wear so it appears they've got bigger tits. I look at Debbie's — small, immature bumps — and agree that yes, she needs the fake boost in those inside pockets of her bra.

Heat rushes to my face, anger asking to come and live inside me, and I let it in, my guest forging through my veins, propelling me to stand and decorate the mannequin with Debbie's clothing, giblets and all. Her phone is in the pocket of her jacket, and I lay it in the mannequin's upturned hand, its arm raised in supplication. Then I drag Debbie to my metal table, lifting her slight frame and placing her in the centre, the hacked-off fingertips and thumb resting between her legs.

I put a couple of things on her.

One is pretty. One isn't.

The table has poles at each corner that reach to the ceiling, and I tie Debbie's wrists and ankles to it — she's not going any-fucking-where.

I stare at her, the scent of drying piss getting a tad ripe. Not exactly something you want to

180

smell of an evening, is it. She was my type once, someone I was praying to turn sixteen, but things are different now, and she won't *ever* be sixteen. Always young, her gravestone will probably say, gone too soon, forever in our hearts.

Forever a hair-sucking pain up my arse.

I sit on the edge of the table, mulling over the memory of her arriving here earlier. I'd been watching the street to make sure no one was about. She'd run up the path. When I'd opened my front door, she'd pressed herself into the dark corner of my front porch. I doubt very much anyone saw her, but you can't be too careful, can you. All it takes is someone putting a rubbish bag in their wheelie bin out the front, hearing footsteps and seeing her trotting along.

I can't think about that now.

A ringing has me jumping, edgy, off-kilter. It's coming from the corner, so I go over there and, bugger me, it's Debbie's phone. The screen is alight, and a dark strip across the centre has writing on it: ALARM. GO HOME.

Well, this could be a bit awkward, couldn't it.

I swipe across the strip, silencing the racket, and consider how long it'll be before her parents start panicking when she doesn't turn up. An hour? Two?

My stomach rumbles — all that hard work has got me hungry — so I collect the steel panel remote from the wall shelf beside where the door hides. I press a button to open the panel, then I'm through the doorway, stepping outside into the crisp air, thankful it smells clean and not like some kitten's litter tray like it does in the den. I secure my little hideaway, press the CLOSE button on the remote. The hum and shuffle of the panel easing into place eases my nerves a bit.

If she wakes and screams, no one will hear her.

Sorted.

TWENTY-ONE

Charlotte roused to the blare of a phone ringing. Groggy, she fumbled for the lamp on the bedside table and couldn't find it. She frowned, propped herself on her elbow, and patted for the lamp base, eyes still closed. The phone trilled on, so she opened her eyes, realising it was *hers*, the screen light casting a rectangular blue beam upwards, illuminating the bedside cabinet a little, showing there wasn't a lamp because this wasn't her bedroom, it was Kane's spare.

Dread poured into her. The only people who had her phone number were Jez and Henry.

Should she answer it or go and find Kane?

Kane had said, after she'd declared she was knackered and needed her bed—in reality, she'd wanted to be alone—he was tired, too, and hoped he'd sleep right through until morning.

She glanced at the clock on the other bedside cabinet. Just after midnight.

No, she wouldn't wake him.

The ringing stopped, and she blew out a shaky breath, her neck throbbing at the pulse point. With Jez out of the nick, it was bound to be him contacting her. She was surprised he'd left it this long, though. Or maybe he didn't even miss her. It wasn't like he'd seen her much when she'd lived there.

Her phone screen went black. She sighed, hands sweating, chills sweeping over her. She imagined he'd be angry she hadn't answered— he'd never stop to think her phone might have been taken away for her safety by the police, to fit with Kane's cover story, monitoring any calls in case the fictious note-writing killer tried to get hold of her.

She settled back in bed, wide awake now— fright was a sod for doing that—and stared into the darkness. Then she closed her eyes, thinking if she breathed deep and listened to the sound of the air sawing in and out of her, she'd fall asleep.

A rattle had her eyes springing open, and she stifled a scream by shoving her fist to her mouth, biting on the knuckles. What the hell was *that*?

It came again, to her left, and she swivelled her head to face the window. Then a single *ping*, another then another, followed by a scattering noise, stone or gravel falling and hitting concrete, and she knew what it was.

Someone throwing stones at the window.

Fuck…

She got up, her legs seeming hollow, and managed to slip-slide to the window over the laminate flooring, her fluffy bed socks easing her way. She stood to the side and moved the curtain across an inch or so and peered out. It was murky, the high hedge creating more darkness than there would be had it not been there, but she made out a face, a hovering oval in the blackness, as if it didn't have a body attached.

She shivered, dropped the curtain, and backed away.

She should wake Kane.

At the door, she pressed the handle down.

Her phone rang again.

"Oh God. Oh God…" she whispered. "Go away. Please, just leave me alone."

The person in the front garden coupled with Jez ringing her was too much, mental overload, and she dashed to the bed, throwing herself under the covers, a little girl again, hiding beneath the quilt, the cover protecting her from the bogeyman.

The ringing went on and on, and if she didn't shut it up, it would get Kane up. She stretched her hand out from beneath her tent and slapped about for her mobile. In her hand, it vibrated, the sensation bringing the ridiculous thought to mind that *his* badness was in that vibration, touching her, burrowing through her skin to infect her inside. Bringing the phone into her hideaway, she stared at the screen with JEZ on a blue stripe and his image underneath.

The sight of him had her retching.

She took a deep breath.

Pressed the ACCEPT CALL button.

Held the phone to her ear.

"I know where you are, Char," he said.

And his voice, his tone, it sent a spiral of nausea through her. She let out an involuntary whimper, and he laughed in two places at once—in her ear and faintly somewhere else…outside…outside in the front garden?

Her stomach rolled over.

How the hell had he worked out where she was? Was the taxi driver one of his mates or something? Fuck, she should have had him drop her in the next street instead.

"I told you, Char, I'll always find you."

The relative safety of the past twenty-four hours melted away, ice in the sun, creating a puddle of regret. She wanted to shout at him, to tell him to fuck the hell off, and she would have had he not been outside. She'd known, when she'd been at the window, that the hovering face was his, but she'd refused to entertain it as anything that could be real.

"You need to go home," she whispered. "You could lead the killer to me."

That sounded stupid — like Jez would be worried about a killer, for God's sake — but it was all she could come up with.

"And the police are here with me," she said. "If they know you're here…"

"I don't give a fiddler's fuck, love. Outside. Now."

"I can't. I'm not allowed." Her throat threatened to close, unshed tears not far away, and she swallowed — dry, so dry — and swiped a hand over her cheek. Tears she hadn't realised were there dampened her palm.

"If you don't come out, I'm going to your mum's."

Bastard. You're such a bastard.

Was it just a threat? Could she risk it?

"I need to get dressed," she said. It would give her some time to think.

"Don't take too long about it. Five minutes, then I'm off to your mother's."

The call ended.

She shoved the quilt off her, too hot now, adrenaline slinking into her system, slowly at first, then racing around. She got up and ran for the door, yanking it back and flying out onto the landing. With no idea which room was Kane's, she peered into each one as she passed. All were empty so far, and at the last one, she stared at a bed with rumpled sheets.

And no Kane between them.

Where was he? Already investigating having heard the stones at the window?

She raced down the steps, skidding at the bottom, gripping the newel post to swing herself around.

The living room — empty.

The kitchen — empty.

Ohfuckohfuckohfuck…

Tempted to turn on the lights to see if she just hadn't seen Kane in her panic, she decided against it, the darkness giving her some kind of protection somehow, as though if she couldn't see Jez outside, he shouldn't be allowed to see her silhouette inside through the curtains.

She breathed deep and walked the kitchen pace by pace, slowly, looking intently into every corner. Then the living room. The hallway. Back up the stairs. Into each room, finally ending up in hers.

Her phone screen lit up with that bright rectangular beam again a second before the ringing blasted out. It seemed so loud, so JEZ IS CALLING, and she let out a yelp, lunging for it then jabbing her finger to answer, raising it to her ear.

She ran back downstairs, thinking to escape via the back way, his silence on the other end ominous. She took a deep breath in the hallway, then...

"Time's up, Char. I'm coming for you."

TWENTY-TWO

Kane stood in the living room of a house that should have had a teenage daughter in it but didn't. Debbie Vine hadn't come home this evening at ten when she usually did, and her parents had called the police at eleven after contacting Debbie's friends to find out she hadn't met them at the park as planned—because she was meeting a new boyfriend instead.

The mother, Ursula, hunched on a black suede sofa with a balled-up Kleenex in her fist, her eyes red and puffy, her bottom lip quivering. Her husband, Xavier, sat beside her, pressed close, his arm across her back, fingers curled over the top of her shoulder. A pitiful pair, two people distraught, their guts undoubtedly churning, nerves strung tight, their world crumbling, nothing they could do about it.

Kane sat on the edge of a chair opposite, Alastair standing by the living room door to his left, notebook in hand, instead of Richard, who hadn't answered his phone when Kane had telephoned him after getting the call from Chief Winter about Debbie going missing. Richard was probably out of it after a date with the bottle. No surprise there.

"Some of these questions may be uncomfortable, and I'm sorry, but I need to ask them." Kane smiled, sympathetic, and hoped the mother would hold up during the interview. Her mind would be all over the place, full of unsettling images, scenarios no mother wanted to imagine, but he couldn't *not* ask.

Standard procedure didn't give a shit about emotions.

"It's fine," Xavier said. "Anything to help." He bobbed his head several times as though giving extra confirmation.

Kane cleared his throat, glad he didn't have or want kids. Glad he'd never have to go through this terror. "You've said you weren't aware of Debbie having a boyfriend. Is she the type to have said so?"

"Yes," Ursula said. "She's already been going on about Ben—a friend of hers; he's one of the lads she was meant to be with tonight. She's had a thing for him...God, got to be coming on two years now. She was going to ask him out this evening. She told us that at dinner, didn't she, Xav?" She looked at her husband.

He nodded. "She did, so for Ben and the others to say she was meeting a different lad... Well, it doesn't make sense."

Kane agreed. "No, it doesn't. So...do you know exactly what message she sent to her friends or just the gist of it?"

"I've got it here." Ursula picked her phone up from the arm of the sofa and swiped the screen. "One of the girls sent it to me as a screen shot. It was a group chat. Debbie sent the message, then everyone else replied, but Debbie didn't respond to any of them."

"Alastair, can you send yourself the screenshot, please," Kane said.

Alistair stepped forward to take the phone then returned to his spot by the door.

"Who did she send the message to—their full names, please," Kane asked.

Xavier rattled them off, addresses, too—clearly parents who made sure they knew who their daughter hung out with and where they lived, something they'd undoubtedly done in case such an event as this happened, never thinking it would.

No one ever thought it would.

"Thank you," Kane said. "What I'm interested in is why she wouldn't have said goodbye as usual."

Ursula closed her eyes and shuddered. She opened them again, fresh tears spilling. "I made a joke about her making the tea." The last two words came out as a wail, going up an octave, and she wedged the tissue to her nose, hand shaking.

"What do you mean by that?" Kane asked.

"She offered to make us a cup of tea," Xavier supplied. "She's never done it before, it's out of the ordinary, and Ursula cracked a quip. You know, like: *What are you after?* It's what you say, isn't it?"

Kane nodded. "How did she react to that?"

"After Ursula pointed out that Deb didn't even know how to *make* tea, Deb stomped off upstairs," Xavier said. "We heard her running a bath, her hair dryer going on. Then she was humming and singing." He swallowed, closed his eyes briefly, swallowed again. "So we were relieved—she wasn't *that* angry if she was singing, was she? We thought she was all right. We thought…"

"Okay. So she didn't leave angry—although she didn't speak, she just left. Did you see her leave?"

Xavier shook his head. "No. Just heard the door shut. By the time I got up and went into the hallway to open it, the street was empty."

Kane nodded absently. "So it's possible no one else saw her either…"

Ursula let out a choked sob. "*Someone* must have. Look at how everyone was out there over Mrs Smithson…or gawping out of their windows. One of them will have seen Deb, won't they? *Please* say they did."

Kane couldn't, and he cringed at what he was about to ask. "This one might be difficult." He paused. "Do you know whether Debbie was sexually active? I ask because teens and sex…they mistake it for love, and it's a strong motivator to do things they wouldn't ordinarily do."

He waited for the outburst of: *No, what a terrible thing to say! What kind of girl do you think she is?*

It never came.

"I'm not sure," Ursula said. "I'd like to say no, but you don't know with kids these days, do you. The friends she meets with — from what I've seen they're good kids, don't get into any trouble, so I'd say none of them are experimenting yet. But...this new boyfriend... I just don't know. And the worst of it is, I wanted to be the sort of mother my child told these things to, knowing she didn't need to be embarrassed, that I'm here for her no matter what, and if she's having sex and didn't tell me... I've failed."

"No, sweetheart," Xavier said, squeezing her to him. "Kids are secretive. We were, remember? They keep things hidden." He looked at Kane. "Clearly."

Normally, in this situation, the questions Kane was asking would fall to uniforms, who would also check the house and garden to see if the missing person was hiding somewhere — or had *been* hidden — but in light of Mrs Smithson being murdered in the same street, Winter had asked Kane to attend the initial questioning.

The invented letter to Charlotte... The wry thought strolled into his head in heavy size tens that maybe he'd tempted fate — that a second neighbour was possibly now in trouble. Or maybe Debbie had just got caught up with her new boyfriend and was testing the boundaries. The fact her phone wasn't being answered, though—that bothered him. But it could just be she'd switched it off, rebellious. After all, what her parents and any other adult might think of as a simple joke about the tea could be a massive slight to a teen. Hormones, discovering their identity, searching for who they were meant to be while the younger, more child-like part of them still whispered inside…it was a heavy burden, growing up.

"Yes, they do keep things to themselves somewhat," Kane said. "I'd like to be able to reassure you that she'll be back, come creeping in soon, hoping you're asleep, but considering what's happened recently… I hate to have to add to your upset, but I need you to have full disclosure and require you to keep it to yourselves. We're trained not to say anything unless absolutely necessary, but I'm not a fan of giving false hope, and with Debbie going missing…" Winter would probably skin him alive for this, but… "Uh, Mrs Smithson didn't kill herself. She was murdered."

"Um, sir?" Alistair said.

Kane ignored him.

Ursula groaned, deep and long and soul-wrenching, and the sound reverberated through Kane, seeming to transfer her distress into him. His heart *hurt*, and he gritted his teeth to stop himself letting out a similar noise.

"We have to consider the fact that someone might…" He couldn't go on. Shouldn't have said anything in the first place, could have gouged his eyes out in remorse, but it was too damn late, his words were hanging there, and this couple who had held on to hope now faced the possibility that their daughter was never coming home. Wasn't it better to face that head-on, though, instead of believing Debbie would waltz in, angry and defiant, saying: *So what if I'm late? So. Fucking. What?*

That would be preferable, but it didn't always happen that way.

"Thank you for being honest," Xavier said. "We…I prefer that."

Kane blew out a rush of air in relief.

"What happens next?" Ursula whispered, fiddling with the tissue.

"House-to-house is ongoing as we speak. There's only one officer out there doing that, so bear with us. We'll let you know of any developments as soon as we can. For now, stay home. Sit tight. Inform me immediately if Debbie makes contact." He reached across and handed Xavier his card. "If you can give Alistair her mobile number, we'll run a check, see if we can get a ping on its location—but that can, unfortunately, take some time." Kane rose. "If you can give Alastair any devices she used—laptop, iPad and the like—we'll see if we can get anything from them. Instant messages et cetera. Did she have Facebook, Twitter, Instagram, Snapchat?"

Xavier nodded. "All of them. MeWe as well. We're on them, too." He went on to give Alastair Debbie's screen names for each one.

After establishing there wasn't a computer the whole family had access to—each member had their own laptop, the parents willing to release theirs as well as Debbie's—Kane said, "Thank you for your time. And I'm sorry to have given such blunt news." He turned to Alastair. "If you can get Debbie's mobile number?"

"Sir." Alastair handed the phone back to Ursula, who pressed buttons, scrolled again, then gave it back. "The network—which network is she with, Mrs Vine?"

"O2," she whispered. "Oh God, this is such a nightmare..." She leant into Xavier, burying her face in his chest, her moans and sobs muffled by his patterned navy-blue jumper.

Kane nodded at Xavier and left the room.

Outside, he stared at the sky, wondering why the hell things like this had to happen.

TWENTY-THREE

Charlotte couldn't bear to open her eyes. She sensed a light was on. The back of her head throbbed. Last she remembered, she'd gone to bed after finishing a glass of wine. She hadn't had a hangover like this since she'd first met Jez, when they'd been young and cider was the alcohol of choice to get rat-arsed on.

She rolled onto her side, and her skull seemed to tighten, clamping around her brain, squeezing in tandem with her heartbeat. Reaching behind, she touched the sore spot—and found a wet patch. She opened her eyes, brought her hand to her face.

Red coated her fingertips.

What?

She sat, staring at her hand, then peered over her shoulder at the pillow. Red soaked the pristine white pillowcase, a deep, dark patch in the centre, scuffs branching off it where she must have shifted in her sleep.

She jolted.

White pillowcase.

The one she'd fallen asleep on had been dove grey—Kane's spare bedding was *grey*.

She bolted out of bed, taking in the room. This wasn't decorated by a man. This didn't have black bedside cabinets that matched the black leather headboard. This was the opposite, white, everything so white, and her heart sank, fear creeping in at the edges, laying down its promise that soon, if she didn't control it, it would overtake her, consume her, and she'd be unable to function.

She was in the place she'd once called home.

Memories flashed, and she remembered.

Jez smashing the glass in the back door of Kane's kitchen.

Charlotte jumping, screaming, rushing upstairs, into her room.

Slamming the door and turning to twist the key, only to find there wasn't a lock.

Pressing her back to the door, planting her feet firmly so if he pushed from the other side, she could hold him off.

Her failing, Jez barging his way in, the door scooting her in an arc—damn her fluffy socks—until she faced one end of the mirrored, built-in wardrobes.

Seeing herself from head to toe, eyes wide, mouth apart, the inside a dark circle in her pale face.

Jez peering round the door, his cheek pressed to the edge, staring at her reflection, a grin showcasing their matching teeth.

Her screaming again, praying the neighbours would hear her and call the police.

Him grabbing her hair, twisting it around his hand—*Kane did that in the hotel*—and dragging her to the bed.

Landing on the mattress, bouncing, then a crack on the back of her head, pain searing, her roar of agony muffled from the covers suffocating her then—

Nothing.

So he'd taken her home, he'd come for her as he'd always promised, and here she was, standing in the bedroom she'd once believed would be their love nest, the place they'd create children, only for it to turn into a mainly sexless relationship and a barren womb, her dreams crushed along with her spirit, her self-confidence, her every-damn-thing.

Anger sent a lance spearing through her, and she choked on the injustices climbing up her throat as words she wanted to spew at him. He had tried to break her, and at one point she'd thought he had, but now she knew different. She'd been isolated, had lived inside the dream he'd planted in her head as a teenager and nurtured until she'd fallen into his web and hadn't been able to climb out, stuck there, the fly, him spinning her into a cocoon, leaving her trapped, helpless, waiting to be devoured.

Never. She wasn't the same person anymore. She might still be broken, but she could fix herself, become a new version, one who'd never take another man's crap, who could stand up for herself and make sure everyone knew she mattered, her life and needs mattered. She'd build new dreams, paper over the cracks of her shattered former self, live a life on her terms, and maybe she wouldn't ever trust another man or have a baby bloating her belly, but at least she'd be free.

She lunged for the door, then remembered this was Jez she was dealing with. Stealth, silence, and recalling every place the floorboards and stairs creaked was needed, ensuring she made it downstairs without a sound. She headed out of the room into the dark, the air humming with silence. Crept along the landing. Down the first three steps in the centre, a step to the right on the fourth, two steps to the left on the fifth. The centre again for the next few, then near the bottom, jumping over the last one — there wasn't anywhere she could tread on it where it wouldn't give her away.

Standing beside the hallway table, she listened, strained to make out where he was. Darkness abounded here, too, except for a thin frame of light around the closed kitchen door. So he was in there, was he, probably having a stiff drink to further bolster his anger — and he *would* be angry at having to come and get her, to bring her home, where he said she belonged.

She wanted to storm in there, demand to know how he'd found her, insist that he got on with his life without her, that she'd had a taste of another man — *yes, another man, Jez, and he was good, so fucking good, and that burns, doesn't it?* — and a taste of life without him, and she loved it, had experienced a sense of peace wrapped inside the constant fear for the first time in years. That she didn't need him, she never had — she knew that now, hindsight lighting up her former dreams as stupid, naïve, childish, a flashing neon light, the word FOOL blinking, flickering, then winking out, because she wasn't a fool, not anymore.

But her venomous, hurtful truths weren't going to come out of her mouth. Not when escape was within reach.

She edged closer to the front door.

Twisted the key.

Curled her fingers around the handle.

Pressed it down.

Flung the door open.

And shrieked at the sound of the alarm going off.

Shit. Oh God. Oh no. Shit!

She looked back at the kitchen door, panicked, expecting to see him standing there, but he wasn't, oh thank God, he wasn't. She turned to face the street, leaping outside, the piercing, wavering note of the siren exacerbating her headache, ratcheting the torture up a notch. She ran, the path gravel digging into her feet, her socks barely any protection, and stubbed her toe on one of those sodding decorative stone balls. She bit back a whine of pain-induced fury, getting to the gate at the same time the alarm silenced.

No. No. He's by the front door. At the alarm panel. So close. Too close.

Out of breath, adrenaline spiking to the point she battled with vomit clawing its way up to her throat, she wrenched the gate inwards, the hinges silent—*there's that WD40 at work again*—cursing as it meant she had to take two steps backwards to enable it to fully open.

He was there. She sensed him behind her a millisecond before he gripped her hair and dragged her in reverse up the path. She opened her mouth to scream, but he clamped his free hand over it, his thumb so close to her nostrils she could barely draw in air. Struggling, she raised her hands above her head then behind, gripping his face, curling her fingertips around the sides of his skull and digging her thumbs into his eyes. The sensation against her skin of round eyeballs and gloop had a smile forming, and she gritted her teeth and dug deeper, pressing to the tune of: *You. Fucking. Bastard!*

The reverberation from his growl rumbled on her back, shuddered through her, and again he was a part of her, inside her, poisoning, souring, tainting. And then his hand was gone from her face, and she gasped, sucked in the cool night air. He let her hair go, and she pushed forward, the ends snagging on his fingertips. Then was free, running, running, running, across the road to Henry's, the only place she'd be safe now until the police arrived.

She whacked on his door, both palms stinging, her throat tight from shock mixed with dogged determination, a mewl coming out of her instead of the scream she intended it to be.

One peek over her shoulder, and she was almost undone. Jez lumbered over the road, heading for her, his face set in a hideous expression, one she'd seen before — the one that meant he was so filled with rage he had it in him to kill her.

She bashed at the door again, whispering, "Please, please, please let me in," and choked on the words, her throat closing, swelling.

"Oi!" Jez shouted, arms bowed at his sides, his biceps and shoulders tensed. "Get the fuck back home."

She whimpered, weakening — her body, her strength, but never her resolve. No, never that. Smacking at the door, frantic, she kicked it, too, her toes cracking, agony shooting through her foot and up her shins.

"Everything all right, sir?" someone said.

She frowned, momentarily stunned, and ceased her assault on the door.

A uniformed policeman strode over from where he'd stood at the Vine's gate, towards Jez, his hand on a baton dangling from a belt at his waist.

"Yeah," Jez said. "The missus is being a nightmare. We had a row. Now piss off."

"Let's have a chat about this, sir, shall we?" the policeman said. "See if we can sort this out."

Then the door opened, and she fell inside the place that had always been her sanctuary, sensing a faint coming on, rising from her toes until it reached her head. She registered Henry's long-sleeved black top, then down she went, her temple slapping onto the hallway floor—*blood flecks on Jez's temple*—nausea swirling, her whole world going dark.

TWENTY-FOUR

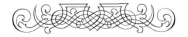

Debbie woke from a nightmare of what had not long happened, the images stark and vivid, reliving it exactly as it had played out. Her eyelids, so heavy, refused to open, stuck there. Everything was too much effort. Thinking, moving, breathing. She drifted in and out of that place where reality merged into dreamland, her subconscious hovering there, teasing, taunting, promising to drag her back to the horror imprinted into her brain, to play it over and over again until she woke once more, drenched in sweat and screaming.

It pulled her under now, that place, and she saw herself in his special room at the bottom of the garden, asleep, her body still, the pain gone while she slumbered in the realm called OBLIVION: WHERE NOTHING HURTS. It was like watching a movie, and she stared, fascinated, breath held at what would happen next, knowing the endless, repeating loop of what she'd been through so very recently would start up again.

And it did.

An unseen hand pressed PLAY, and there was nothing she could do but observe.

She woke in the darkness, her position a star shape, the same way as she slept at home. So, it had just been a nightmare then, her going to his house and being taken into his summer house. She breathed out in relief, thankful she wasn't still there, him with that creepy-arsed wig on, talking with someone else's voice. She went to curl her arms around herself, but they wouldn't move. Panicked, she tugged, and her whole body chilled from the outside in.

Something's wrong.

"Mum?" she called, fear rising, manifesting as a ripple in her solar plexus that exploded up into her chest, constricting her lungs, cutting off her ability to breathe.

She writhed, her shoulders rising then falling to hit a hard surface — she wasn't in her bed, wasn't in her bedroom with the pink-patterned wallpaper and the framed poster of Ed above her head. At the point she thought her lungs would burst, they relaxed, and she sucked in air — air that smelt of dried piss — and remembered blacking out as she'd wet herself, the wee hot on her skin, trickling into her Converses, creeping beneath her feet.

So she *had* gone to his house, she was *still* there, and everything she'd thought was a dream was her new reality.

Debbie whimpered, her mind working overtime as she tried to figure a way out of this mess. He wasn't her fantasy man, he was her worst enemy, and she'd bet it was way past ten now, her curfew long gone. Mum and Dad would be crapping themselves about her not coming home. Not angry, no, not that, just scared and worried about where she was.

She wished she'd told them where she was going and again wished she'd said goodbye. What if she didn't get out of here? What if he was here, standing close by, ready to snuff her life out?

Listening hard, she couldn't detect any breathing but her own. No other sounds except her ragged inhales and exhales and the speeding thump of her heartbeat, the click of her dry throat when she swallowed.

"Help me!" she shouted. "Someone help me!"

There was a *whoosh* then a metallic click — something sliding into place? A soft whine, a rustling, leaves maybe, some shuffling, then three footsteps, another click, and the *whoosh* again, punctuated with a third click.

"Who's there?" Stupid, such a *stupid* thing to say. Like he was going to answer her.

If it was him.

"Quiet," he said.

She shook, fear taking on a new meaning, everything about her cold and slimy, sweat breaking out on her forehead to dribble down her temple and into the shell of her ear, icy, bringing on a sweeping shiver. Her teeth chattered, and she clamped them together, but it didn't do anything to stop it. Wet heat flooded between her legs, slithered beneath her backside, chilling quickly.

"You were naughty earlier," he said.

And he was right beside her, she sensed it. How had he been so silent when walking over to her? She wished she could see, to gauge his facial expression and what might be coming next, then she hoped she could stay in this darkness, blind to whatever the hell was going on around her.

"I want my mum," she said—and she did, God she did, more than anything in the world.

"Too late for that," he said. "You didn't act the way you should have. You upset my sister. I can't have my sister upset."

Was she here, his sister, standing somewhere in this infinite blackness?

"I did-didn't mean it." Her stuttering brought home just how scared she was, how young, how ridiculous she'd been to think he was interested in her, in building a life together, their love story being told for generations to come, how the younger girl and the older man had fallen in love despite the odds, despite the warnings that it would never work.

"Apologies are supposed to be heartfelt," he said. "You don't *sound* sorry."

"But I am," she said, hating the whine in her voice, the way she'd shown her age, how petrified she was. "Here, listen: I'm sorry, I'm sorry, I'm *sorry*!"

"Now you're just being facetious."

What does that mean?

"I'm not, I swear. I'm sorry—really. Please. Let me go home. I won't tell anyone what happened, I promise. I'll just pretend I stayed out late, and no one will ever know where I was, and I'll never come here again or speak to you, so no one will suspect you of anything."

"The lady doth protest too much, methinks," he said.

Hamlet. God, she'd do anything to be reading that, Miss Boring as Fuck warbling on, raising her voice at Debbie to *listen*, to pay *attention*, will you?

"No, no, I'm not lying, I'm telling—"

The slap on her leg sucked all the air out of her, and once again she couldn't breathe, couldn't think, couldn't function. Her body went rigid, blackness oozed into the edges of her mind, and if it weren't for wanting to be with Mum, Dad, and Squiggly, she'd die right now, just to get away from him. Then she breathed again, her leg stinging, her chest hurting from how much her heart banged.

"I have to end this," he said. "You could have learnt a lot from me, you know. I said I'd teach you things, didn't I, but you messed it up. Once I've sorted you, I've got Charlotte to deal with. The pair of you are nothing but pests. Fuck's sake…"

"What did I do to deserve this?" she wailed.

A beat of time, another, then, "You sucked your hair."

"I…I don't understand…"

A brilliant blue, orange-tipped flame lit up the darkness, stretched taut by the force of whatever powered it. She gasped, unable to fathom what it was beyond being fire. It rippled and wavered at the top, and the faint vision of his face lurked behind it, pushing away some of the shadows to reveal his mouth and nose. She sucked in a breath, which caught in her throat and tickled, bringing on the urge to cough. She arched her back, yanking at her arms and legs, trying to free them from whatever they were tied to.

Got to get out. Got to go home.

The flame moved towards her, stopping on the right, and it turned in the gloom, the end pointing at her upstretched arm.

"This is going to sting a bit," he said. Chuckled. Belly-laughed.

As the heat bit into her arm, she screamed, the sound infinite, the smell of her singed skin, her melting skin, like Sunday roast pork left in the oven too long. She convulsed, her mind refusing to work, her head filled with nothing except the knowledge of how agonising this torture was.

Then nothing.

She woke to her arms feeling on fire, her legs, too, the pain roaring back into her limbs, the stench of burnt meat overwhelming. She screamed again, but it came out silent, and for a microsecond she acknowledged she'd screeched so much before she'd passed out that her vocal cords now refuse to function.

Then nothing.

Debbie's eyelids fluttered, and she opened her eyes. There was the flame again, so close the heat from it warmed her cheek. When he brought it closer, she knew what he was going to do, that this was the end.

And she welcomed it.

She pulled out of the dream world now, her face, arms, and legs still so hot she imagined they continued cooking even though the flame wasn't there. Her lungs crackled with the effort of breathing, small intakes of air that came out as short, limp puffs. She stared at herself from the outside in, fascinated that her eyes had melted, her lips gone, her teeth exposed, her braces dull silver, her face a red raw…mess.

It wouldn't be long now, and she'd be gone. Away from here at last.

She thought of Mum, of how she'd always said that if anything happened to Debbie, she wouldn't be able to carry on, life wouldn't be worth living. And Dad, how he'd said he'd kill anyone who hurt her, and it was funny, odd, made no sense, but she hoped he didn't go after him—no, Dad needed to make sure he didn't end up in prison for trying to right this terrible wrong.

She thought she was grown up before. She'd been wrong. *Now* she was grown up, mature, and it was too late for her to do anything but wait for that last breath.

It came, seeping into her without any sense of purpose, as if knowing it wouldn't do anything worthwhile. Debbie hoped for Heaven, for peace, and no more pain, and that final exhalation tiptoed out of her, the very core of her snuffing out.

Gone.

TWENTY-FIVE

Charlotte blinked awake, greeted by a darkness so deep it chilled her to the marrow. Disoriented, she mentally checked her body parts, and the only thing that hurt was her head and face. She reached back to feel her skull, the blood dry in places now, her hair hard with it, but a soft, spongy section had her stomach churning. She didn't probe to see

217

how deep the gouge was. She didn't want to know.

Where was she? She'd blacked out from fear in Henry's hallway—she recalled falling, fainting, hitting her temple. She checked it now, patting gingerly, and winced at the sharp pain of a bruise, imagining a purple knot the size of half a golf ball, going by her careful exploration and the shape of the lump.

Then she remembered coming round to the sound of a voice—Jez's—and another. The policeman? Yes, that was right. He'd asked if she was okay, and she'd nodded, then realised that although she was technically all right, she wasn't safe, not with Jez around. Before she'd been able to tell the policeman she needed help, to ask him to contact Kane, a shout had gone up over the road, and he'd run off.

More voices, Jez and Henry talking.

'I'll deal with her.'

'Are you sure?'

'Of course I'm fucking sure.'

Then sweet oblivion.

Now this never-ending blackness and no idea where she was. No idea which one of them had said they'd take care of her, as their voices had blurred, floated off, her not able to work out who had said what.

She sniffed, her nostrils assaulted by the scent of something burnt. Was she in the kitchen at

Jez's, the smell lingering from where he'd tried to cook something in her absence? Whatever it was, it had been singed to a crisp, and her stomach contracted at the strength of the odour.

Charlotte managed to stand, going a little dizzy, her head spinning, and she felt sick. She reached out in an attempt to feel her way across the space, and her hand brushed the corner of something. Sharp, it scratched the undersides of her fingers. She hissed, clenched her teeth, waited for the sting to pass. A moment slipped by, segueing into another and another and so many more after that. She steadied herself and patted around for that corner again, smoothing her fingers over something cold until a hard, lumpy surface halted her exploration. She felt it, moved her fingers along it, and it reminded her of how the dried-out part of her head had felt.

Her stomach churned.

She moaned, and it sounded so unlike her she wondered if it was someone else. Was she even alone? Had Jez been the one to take her, locking her up somewhere, sitting in the corner now, waiting?

She shuffled away from that…thing she'd touched, hands out in front of her, and came to what she assumed was a wall. She pressed her palms to it, walking sideways, to the right, waiting to reach a window frame, a door, anything to give her hope. Her pinky bumped into what she guessed was plastic, and she ghosted her hand farther across.

A light switch.

She pressed it and blinked in the harsh brightness, seeing nothing for a good while. It took several seconds for her vision to adjust, and then she stared at a metal wall. Confused — *where the hell am I?* — she spun to face the other way.

And wished she hadn't.

A body — *oh God, a burnt body* — rested on a metal table, unmoving, and she knew then that was what she'd touched, that charred flesh, that hard and lumpy surface she'd likened to the gash on her head. She retched, slapping her hand over her mouth, and squeezed her eyes shut.

If she opened them, the body would be gone, and she'd laugh because this wasn't happening, it had been a figment of her imagination. Hadn't it? Wasn't that the way this was going to go? It was, because this sort of thing didn't happen, not in this town, her world. Except it did — *Mrs Smithson* — and Charlotte dreaded facing this nightmare she'd found herself in.

So don't open your eyes then.

She ignored herself, of course she did, opening them — *the body's still there, still there, still there, oh my God* — and looked around in panic for a door, a window, some way to escape. But she was in what amounted to a metal-lined box, a room, with that steel table, a desk, a filing cabinet, a huge wooden wardrobe, and—

What?

What?

A mannequin in the corner.

Her life had turned into a nightmare, and living with Jez, enduring all she had at his hands, paled by comparison. Charlotte shuddered, one that racked her whole frame, her nerves strung taut, and she rushed to the body, thinking to check for signs of life but knowing it was futile. Whoever this person was, they were long gone, their torment over.

She took in the limbs, so wrecked, and the face—no features, no eyes—the torso unmarked, a cerise bra covering the small breasts.

A cerise bra…

No.

No, it couldn't be. It had been in her bag—she'd put it there in the hotel, and it had still been there when Henry had given her the mail, then her bag had fallen from the seat in the taxi, and that man had picked it up and…

What was it *doing* here?

Had the man *stolen* it?

She choked on a sob, gasping for air, her mind clouding from lack of oxygen. Grey shadows converged at the edge of her vision, growing by the second, eventually obliterating her sight until she stared at blackness again. She fell and sank into the abyss which pulled her down, her conscious mind shutting off, leaving a void behind.

She'd been awake, nosing about, inquisitive, but now the dopey tart's out of it again. Prone to fainting, that one. Her curled-up image is grainy on my phone, but it's best I watch her from here. Can't be doing with being bored in the den, waiting for her to wake up.

Someone's knocking at the door, and I've half a mind to ignore it. Normally I would, but with things going on in the street tonight, down at the Vine house, I'll be better off showing my face, letting people know I'm around. That I can't possibly have taken Debbie.

Hahaha.

I switch off the camera app and slip my mobile into my pocket. Glance around to make sure everything's looking okay, then make my way to the door. I turn on the outside light then swing the door inwards, schooling my expression to one of confusion as to why someone would be calling at this time of the morning. I mean, come on, it's past two o'clock.

A copper stands there, the same one from earlier, the one who'd gone knocking on doors about Debbie, then had come back again to help Charlotte, running off when Xavier had called him for help. Ursula had fainted apparently—*what is it with women doing that?*—and Xavier was worried she'd done herself some damage.

"All right?" I say, raising my eyebrows. "Found Debbie, have you?"

"Err, no. Sorry to knock so late, but I saw your light on. Just checking in about earlier. About the lady. Everything still okay?"

"As far as I know, yeah."

"Is the lady in bed?"

"No idea, mate."

He frowns. "Oh. Right. Uh…" He blinks, like he isn't sure what to say next.

"What I mean is, she isn't here. Isn't in this house. Come in and have a look if you like." I step back, hold my arm out to let him know he's welcome to check.

He nods, as if to himself, like he's working out whether he ought to enter without having a pig buddy with him.

"I don't bite," I say, then laugh. "I'll wait outside if you want. I get that you might be wary, what with Mrs Smithson being…well, you know, and Debbie staying out late." I move into the front garden and stand there, arms out to my sides, a gesture that says: It's all right, I'm not

223

bothered. "Go on in. Shut the door behind you. I can't get back in then — keys are indoors, see."

He stares at me, and I wonder if I've gone a bit too far. You know, hammed it up above and beyond the norm. But he smiles. Steps in the house. Closes the door. And I stay here, hoping he doesn't feel the need to go out into the back garden. Then again, the trees in front of the den are thick fuckers, and you can't see through them; they're planted too close together for that.

He's back quick sharp, his figure behind the glass in the door, then he's out on the path with me, smiling again. "Thanks. No one's home."

"No. Like I said, she's not in the house. So if that's all?"

"Yes. Right, goodnight then."

"Night."

I go inside, close the door, and I don't hesitate in the hallway — he might be watching for that. In the living room, I sit and count to one thousand, then pull my phone out and access the app.

Ah, she's awake.

Good.

I slip into protective clothing — might be a bit of spraying blood in my future — pick up an old sock off the pile of washing on the kitchen side, lift a balaclava from the hook beside the back door, and leave the house.

Charlotte sucked in a breath at the weird whirring noise. A metal panel pushed out of the wall opposite and slid to the right, revealing a uPVC door with no windows. Her heart thudded so hard, and she scrabbled to her feet, intent on rushing at whoever came in, racing towards the opening as it got wider and wider.

A man entered, an orange boiler suit fitted over his bulky frame, face covered with a black woolly balaclava, only his eyes and mouth visible — and the lower half of a moustache. Fear clutched at her heart, but she surged closer, survival her only goal.

He spotted her and lunged forward, grabbing her around the waist then kicking the door closed. She struggled, fought his hold, but he spun her around, and as she widened her mouth to scream, he shoved material inside it. She retched, tasting the scent of fabric softener — *Lenor, it's yellow Lenor* — instinctively sucking in a breath, resulting in the material going farther in, touching the back of her throat. She panicked, moving her tongue repeatedly to shift whatever it was forward. Sniffing in oxygen, relieved she could breathe, she jabbed her foot back, hoping to connect with his shin but instead her sole met with air.

He dragged her to the wardrobe and flung her down in front of one of the doors. The momentum had her head flying back, hitting the wood, and fresh pain flowered in her wound. The other wardrobe door creaked open, and an arm flopped out—an arm covered in Henry's long-sleeved black top.

Oh God, no. Please, not Henry. Don't tell me that's Henry in there.

She shuffled away on her arse, desperate for distance. The man prodded a button on a fob, and the metal panel hummed and moved. She pulled the material out of her mouth and gulped in enough air to launch a scream, but he sank to his knees and covered her mouth with his hand.

"Shh!"

She shivered, absolute terror flooding her system, the need to pee so strong she didn't know if she could resist. To take her mind off it, she tried to bite his hand, but he tented it, her efforts pointless. The metal panel clicked into place, and he whipped his hand away and stood. She jumped to her feet, adrenaline giving her energy, and lashed out, grabbing the balaclava and wrenching it off, ready to give Jez what for but—

It. Wasn't. Him.

TWENTY-SIX

There wasn't much more Kane could do now other than go home. He had hung around at the station while specially trained officers had accessed Debbie's, Ursula's, and Xavier's devices. Nothing of interest on the parents', and the only thing on Debbie's was the notes she'd written in Word, saved in a folder labelled FANTASY MAN.

They'd gleaned this new boyfriend was older than her — significantly so — and that if it wouldn't be such a problem for her mum and dad, she'd have told them about him. There was nothing more she'd like better than to share her love for him with them. One of the pieces had Kane aching like a tooth abscess when he'd read it, and he'd had to walk away from the laptop in order to compose himself.

She was a kid in love. A kid who thought all she had to do was make the boyfriend see how mature she was, and everything would work out fine. She'd listed the date of their future wedding, the children they'd have — one boy, one girl — and their names.

The notes had been printed out several times each so the team all had a copy for at the start of the next shift — several eyes were better than his pair, and maybe someone would pick up something Kane had missed.

On the cusp of leaving and going home, at the last minute, Kane decided to stay and read the notes again. Something was nagging at the back of his mind, and he needed to check one last time, otherwise he wouldn't get any damn sleep from thinking about it.

But Nada strolled in, face showing her lack of sleep — shadows beneath her eyes, mouth pinched — and he remembered he'd sent her and Erica out to question the sex workers. Christ, that seemed ages ago now, as though a week had passed.

"Oh, hello, sir," Nada said, her smile weary. "Didn't expect you to be here." She walked slowly over to her desk and slumped into her chair. "Bloody knackered, I am." She sighed and rubbed her temples. "And it's parky out there. Thought my nipples were going to drop off at one point." She blushed. "Sorry, sir. Forgot it was you I was talking to for a minute."

"Don't worry about it." He smiled. "Why are you here and not at home?"

Nada shrugged. "Didn't see the point, considering the hour. You know it's ten to three, don't you? Only a few hours and it's time to start work again. Thought I'd make myself useful and type up our notes. Erica went home, the lightweight."

She grinned, and he knew he'd done the right thing in suggesting her to Winter as his new partner.

"Find anything out?" he asked. "Anything we can use?"

She bit her bottom lip.

"Come on, out with it," he said. His nerves jangled. Could he handle anything more right now? Should he tell her to can it, wait until tomorrow?

It is tomorrow.

She winced. "Um, it seems one of our own has been frequenting that patch, sir." She pulled a face as if to say "Eek!"

"What?" He frowned, his mind sluggish from lack of sleep. "Patrolling? So what?"

She shook her head.

"Explain."

"Err, Richard has been using prostitutes," she said.

"*What*?" He frowned. Surely not. Richard didn't *like* sex workers. He'd said so only recently. "Pack it in now. You're kidding me, aren't you?"

She shook her head. "Wish I was, but one of them mentioned him by name. Said he'd been there the night one of them got killed — the one found in the warehouse."

"Jesus fucking wept." He blew out a long stream of breath, trying to process the information. Was that why Richard had been acting oddly? Because he'd bloody killed that woman? "Dear God…"

"I know. Sorry." Nada offered a sympathetic smile, but it didn't fix fuck all. "He's your partner, and I wasn't sure what to do."

"No, you did the right thing in telling me. Bloody hell, this was the last thing I expected." He stared at the floor. "Richard, though…"

"That's what I thought. He might be a pisshead, but I never had him down as someone who'd pay for sex, knowing it's, you know, *illegal*." She sniffed. "What will you do? Will you tell Winter, I mean?"

Kane nodded. "Of course, but I'll speak to Richard first, though, give him the chance to come clean to the chief."

His mobile rang in his pocket, startling him. He drew it out, checked the screen: RICHARD.

"Oh, you're having a laugh," he said. "What are the odds?" He glanced at Nada. "It's him."

"Blimey." She got up. "I'll err…give you some privacy."

"No. Stay with me. I'll put it on speaker."

He answered and held the phone up. "Hello?"

"Kane…" Heavy breathing. "I…I need to…tell you something."

Too right you do.

Kane made eye contact with Nada. She did the *eek* face again.

"All right, mate," he said, going for friendly. "What's up?"

"I've done a bad thing…and…and…I'm going to do another bad thing." More heavy breathing.

Fuck. "What bad thing?"

"The…the prostitutes."

"What about them?"

"I shouldn't have… It was wrong. I didn't mean to."

"Didn't mean to what?"

"I can't take this anymore. I'm…I'm so sorry."

A shuffle, something falling, then silence.

"Fucking hell." Kane shot out of his seat and jammed his phone in his pocket. "Come on."

He strode to the door, Nada following, and they raced down the stairs, the soles of their shoes squeaking with every turn on the landings. Out the back entrance, across the car park, and into his car, Nada buckling up while he revved the engine. He sped off, heart going like the clappers, his mind reeling with what he thought had happened. Richard had gone too far with a sex worker and had killed her. Was that why he'd been smoking in the corner at the scene? Had he lit a cigarette after he'd murdered her and wasn't sure if he'd dropped some ash so deliberately let some fall from his fag the next morning?

The duplicity seared Kane's gut. All along, Kane had thought his partner just had a drink problem, when really he'd been shagging people he shouldn't have been shagging, had snuffed out her life, the nameless victim they'd yet to find an identity for. No matter what she'd done for a living, she hadn't deserved that. Hadn't deserved a copper, of all people, someone who was supposed to represent security, safety, to end it the way he had.

"Did you find out her name?" he asked Nada. "The woman he killed?"

"He *killed*? You mean you think *Richard* did her in? Fucking Nora… Whoa, watch it, sir. Nearly hit that bloody bollard then."

"Sorry." He slowed a bit. "I don't know what I think. I just…" He shook his head. "Did you? Did you get a name for her?"

"Yes, a Tammy Weston." She paused. "Uh, where are we going?"

"The warehouse." He swerved down a side street, put his foot down.

"What? You think he's doing it *again*?" she screeched.

"You heard him, didn't you? He said he'd done a bad thing and is going to do another. Got any better ideas as to what that means?"

He pelted down Jude Street, skidding to a stop outside Clarks. He bolted out of the car, running down the alley, the sound of his footsteps merging with Nada's behind him. He headed for the warehouse, cursing to Hell and back that a wooden board had been fixed in front of the door, crime scene tape criss-crossed over it.

He came to a stop, assessing his options, and all he could do was haul himself up onto one of the empty spaces where windows used to be and drop inside. His landing sent pain shooting up his legs, and he scoured the interior of the ground floor.

Nothing and no one.

Up the stairs he went, getting out of breath, his lungs burning from the effort, sweat breaking out on his back. He bypassed the rooms that had been full of rubbish, now cleaned by SOCO, and entered the empty one.

Again, nothing and no one.

"Fuck!" He pulled at his hair. "*Fuck!*"

The adrenaline rush still gallivanting through him, he returned to Nada outside, jerking his head towards the warehouse. "There's jack shit going on in there. Come on."

Back in the car, he headed to Richard's house, lurching to a stop outside the terraced nineteen-twenties property and hauling arse up the flagstone path, almost tripping on a wonky slab. Nada joined him at the door, and he hammered on the glass at the same time as jabbing the bell button.

"Answer, damn it!" He gritted his teeth, smacked at the door again, then leant down to peer through the letterbox. "Aww, shit! *Shit!*"

"What's the matter, sir?" Nada crouched beside him, breath shunting out of her.

Kane moved aside, and Nada looked in.

"Oh God," she said.

So Kane hadn't imagined it.

Richard *was* hanging from a noose attached to the banisters, then.

TWENTY-SEVEN

"**Y**ou!" Charlotte says. "I...I don't understand."

Part of me wants to take the piss out of her whiny voice, to mimic her—*I don't understand, I don't understand; oh, use your brain, you thick bitch*. The amount of times I've had to hear it over the years. Fucking torture.

"What don't you understand, you silly cow? I mean, it isn't difficult, is it? There you are, sitting by a wardrobe with that fuckface of a boyfriend of yours in it, and here I am, standing in front of you, about to do you in. What's not to understand?"

She gasps, her hand whipping up to cover her mouth, and at one time I longed to kiss that mouth, to give her everything, from love to devotion to money to security, but she stuck around with that loser, didn't she, threw my offers of a better life out of the goddamn window, bringing us to this point.

"This is your fault, you know. Us being here like this," I say. "If you'd only listened to what I was *really* saying all this time, this wouldn't be happening."

"What do you mean?"

She wails, and it gets to me. Like, she's dense, got to be, and her not getting it, not understanding, just shows me it would never have worked, me and her.

"Oh, *come off it*," I say. "When a bloke says stuff to you like: I'm always here for you. Don't forget where I am if you need me. You don't have to put up with him, you know, there are men out there who will treat you better… You're telling me that went over your head, that you didn't *twig* what I was saying?"

She blinks. Thick as pig shit, she is.

What did I ever see in her?

"I...I didn't realise you felt that way," she whispers.

"I'm going to have to teach you a lesson." I give her one hard motherfucker of a stare. "Like Smithson and that stupid bint over there."

Her gaze flicks to Debbie, and she winces, tears filling eyes I used to love staring into. "You stole my bra. When I went to the toilet, you took it out of my bag, didn't you."

She's not so dumb after all. I clap slowly. "Well done. Gold star. Fuck's sake...is that all you're bothered about? Your bra? Always were a selfish bitch, Char. Everything was always about you. 'He's done this to me. I can't take it anymore. He hit me. I can't stand him.' Oh, behave your bloody self. Didn't you ever wonder *why* he did those things? Look at you. Look at the state of you."

She does as she's told—finally, after all this time—and I want to slap her for taking sixteen sodding years to obey an order. Jez smacked her around because even when he'd threatened her, she'd still defied him in small ways.

"Yeah, you see it, don't you?" I say. "How do you think Jez felt, starting out his adult life with a young bird who always looked mint, then she turned into Drab Dora, eh? And there was you saying to me, 'He doesn't make love like we used to anymore, and I don't know why.' *That's* why." I point at her clothes. "What you've got on is enough to turn any bloke off. Your hair — what the hell happened to it? Where's the makeup?" I shake my head. "Oh, silly me, I forgot, when you went out to get *milk*, you dolled yourself up then, didn't you. The kind of milk you got wasn't from no cow."

She gasps, and I know I've hit the nail on the head. She was out shagging, wasn't she, the dirty little tramp.

"Thanks a *lot*," I say.

"What?"

"For passing me over. For getting your jollies with someone else, when I've been waiting here all this time. Yeah, thanks a fucking bunch."

"Henry, I—"

"Don't call me that. It's H1 to you."

"H *what*?"

Oh, she's really getting on my wick. "H1. The bloke who's been storing your boyfriend's drug stash all these years, going out of an evening and threatening the punters for him when they don't pay up. That's what *he* does at night and all. Yeah, you might well look at me like that, but your fancy house and everything in it don't come cheap, and neither does mine. How the hell did you think I could live in a poncy house like this when I haven't got a bloody job? Get a fucking clue, will you?"

She whimpers, and I've just about had enough, so I haul her upright, shove her back towards Debbie. I slap her so hard she staggers sideways and falls, goes down like a sack of shit.

Jesus Christ, she's out again, eyes shut, mouth sagging open.

With a bit of luck, she's dead.

If she is, it'll have saved me a job, won't it.

TWENTY-EIGHT

Uniforms waited in the kitchen of Richard's house, and Kane stood beside Nada in the hallway, unable to look at Richard hanging there, at the worn soles of his slippers. He turned away, walking to the door so he could wait outside on the path.

Breathing in the fresh air, he willed it to clear his head, to get some sense of peace in there instead of this boiling mass of questions that had no answers. It hadn't escaped his notice that several people had clocked the activity — someone kicking in a door in the middle of the night would do that, wake you up, get you shuffling to your window; *What the devil is that, love, kids messing about again, is it?* —and he pulled the door to, ensuring they couldn't see inside the house.

He sighed, his mind so full yet numb at the same time, like his brain cells were firing in one half but dead in the other.

A car eased up to the kerb, Gilbert getting out with his trusty black case, and Kane straightened his spine, gave himself a talking to: *Act professional. Don't lose it now.* He felt guilty for moaning about Richard and his drinking, for his partner's lack of attention at work when the man had bigger issues to deal with. The suicide note… God, it had been difficult reading.

I CAN'T GO THROUGH CHEMO. SORRY.

Bloody hell, Kane had had to squeeze his eyes shut at that, recalling the yellow tinge to Richard's skin, thinking his liver was packing up from alcohol, when all along it had likely been cancer, and Richard had probably been drinking to blot out the reality of it, unable to face the diagnosis.

Assume makes an ass out of u and me.

And Kane had assumed all right.

"Deary bloody me," Gilbert said, rocking up the path and coming to a stop in front of Kane. "This is a bit of a shock, isn't it?"

"Just a bit." Kane nodded. "I thought—"

"Don't." Gilbert rested a hand on his shoulder. "We both thought it. And there was you saying I'd be the one to do his postmortem, but I didn't think it'd be this soon."

"It was a joke. I was angry. I shouldn't have opened my mouth. I…"

Gilbert squeezed his shoulder then took his hand away. "Listen, you've put up with a lot of crap off him for a while now. Last two years, isn't it? How were you supposed to know he was ill? Did Winter or Richard ever say anything, give you a heads-up? No, they didn't, so stop blaming yourself."

Kane shook his head. "I should have paid more attention. He'd said he had something going on, something he had to do. What if he left work yesterday to go to some appointment or other and got even worse news?"

"But he didn't tell you, did he, so how can you expect to have helped?"

"I couldn't have."

"Well, then, no remorse." Gilbert smiled. "Richard hadn't been doing his job properly, and you can't carry a crap partner. Harsh but true. You know me, say it how it is. Realist not fantasist. Best way to be, that."

"I grassed him up to Winter," Kane said. "I requested Nada as my new partner. What sort of person does that? Christ."

"A normal person. And so you should have told the boss. Not being funny, but if young Zeb down in the morgue didn't do his fair share, you can bet I wouldn't be putting up with it. He's there to do a job, health issues or not, and if he's not fit to do the work, he shouldn't be there. Same as Richard. He should have retired. He was getting on a bit anyway. No one would have questioned it. Richard dropped the ball when things went to shit."

"He's right there, you know," Kane said. "Right behind us."

"Well, it's not like he can hear me anymore, is it?" Gilbert roared with laughter then snapped his mouth shut. "Oops, forgot it's the early hours and people won't be awake yet." He glanced up and down the row of houses. "Then again, looks like most of them are. Anyway, I've got a job to be getting on with. Your free counselling session is over. It'll cost you the price of a pint in the local next time we're there at the same time. Now get yourself off to bed."

Kane would never get used to Gilbert's humour, his way of dealing with things.

Gilbert went inside, said, "How's it hangin', Rich?" then laughed again. "That joke never gets old."

Kane blocked him out, staring across the street, thinking of Debbie, wondering where she was and whether they'd find her, take her home to her mum and dad. Her parents were likely sitting up right now, wide awake, still fretting, wringing their hands, pacing, blaming themselves.

HE DOESN'T LIVE FAR. I COULD TAKE A FEW STEPS, AND THERE HE'D BE, SMILING AT ME THROUGH HIS WINDOW, WAVING.

"Fuck me sideways..." Kane dashed inside, spotting Nada in the kitchen at the end of the hallway talking to a PC. "Nada!"

She turned her head in his direction. "Boss?"

"We're needed elsewhere."

She bolted out of the room, probably sensing the urgency, and he strode out, down the path, getting into his car and starting it up before she'd even reached the gate. He pressed the accelerator, gesturing to her through the window to hurry the hell up, and she ran around the front of the vehicle and threw herself inside. Then he was off, heading towards the Vine house, desperate to get there quickly so he could pick their brains about the neighbours opposite and find out whether any males lived alone. While speeding along, he searched his mind for information from the neighbours' statements, their names, what they'd said, what they'd seen — or not.

Coming up blank, he smacked the dash, and Nada jumped.

"Bloody hell, boss, do you have to?"

"Sorry," he muttered.

"Mind telling me where we're going and what we're going there for in such a rush? Anyone would think your arse is on fire."

"Debbie Vine's house. Listen, I need some info."

"All right, but remember I'm tired, so there might not be any information readily available." She pulled a Werther's Original out of her pocket and held it towards him. "Want one?"

"No, what I want is for you to work something out for me. Think back to the neighbours' statements regarding Mrs Smithson's murder, okay? I read Debbie's files earlier, ones stored on her laptop, and she wrote: *He doesn't live far. I could take a few steps, and there he'd be, smiling at me through his window, waving.* Who lives alone on the other side of the street, do you know?" He shot Nada a quick look.

She frowned, pressed her fingertips to her forehead, her thumb to her right cheek. "Give me a second or two, will you? I'm a few peas short of a casserole at the minute."

"What?" Kane frowned and riveted his attention on the road ahead.

"You know, I'm a few Fruit Loops shy of a full bowl."

"Whatever you're on, Nada, get off it. *Concentrate.*"

"Sorry, sir."

Tension bunched his muscles, and he focused on breathing and getting to the Vine's in one piece.

"Ah," Nada said. "I remember now. Me and Lara took turns on that side of the street. Everyone I spoke to hadn't seen anything, and they were either female singles or part of a couple. But Erica mentioned a bloke who gave her the creeps. She said he wore all black, had a really bushy moustache that she swore had the remains of his last meal in it. Churned my stomach when she said that."

Kane huffed out an impatient breath.

"Anyway," she went on, "he lives alone, said he'd been at home all night and hadn't seen or heard anything, and…"

He turned to catch her scrunching her eyes up. "And…?"

"I'm trying to visualise the street, sir. Hang on a sec."

Give me strength…

"Yes, right, he lives opposite the Vine family, sir, two doors down from Mrs Smithson."

Kane cheered internally, swerving to miss a tabby cat wandering across the road, yellow eyes gleaming in the glare of the headlights, his instinct telling him this was the man Debbie had been mooning over. He slewed into the street in question, tyres screeching, and glided to a stop outside the Vine's place.

"Name," he demanded, snapping back the lock lever and elbowing open the door.

Nada did the same. "If I remember rightly, Henry Cobber or something."

"Cobbings," he said, the name jangling around in his head, the *ding-ding-ding* of the winner's bell ringing loudly.

He belted up Cobbings' path, moving to the door and crouching. Quietly, he pushed up the letterbox, his recent action of doing the same at Richard's house bringing on goosebumps, but nobody hung here, no feet dangled in red-and-black tartan slippers. The hallway was in darkness except for a sliver of light seeping beneath the door to the right.

He stood, glanced left, eyeing a wooden garden gate attached to the side of the house. It was tall, had to be about six foot, and if he couldn't open it, he'd have to climb over. He turned the old-fashioned ring handle, and the latch on the other side must have lifted, judging by the rusty squeak. But it was still locked, so he reached over the top to feel for a bolt. It was too far down for him to get a grip on it, so he stood side-on to the gate and linked his hands.

"Up you get," he whispered. "Undo the bolt, will you?"

Nada planted her foot in his hands, the sole of her shoe gritty on his skin, and he hoisted her up. The scrape of the bolt moving seemed overly loud, and he cringed. Nada jumped down, and Kane opened the gate, pushing it slowly in case it had a mind to protest the way the bolt had. It didn't, so he led the way down the alley and out onto a smallish lawn.

He frowned. This area wasn't as big as Mrs Smithson's and didn't seem in keeping with her layout. Her garden went farther back, yet this one appeared half the depth. He hauled himself up onto the fence that separated this garden from the one next door. Their space went back another eighteen feet, easy.

Kane jogged towards the trees at the edge of the grass and shoved himself between two of them.

You fucking beauty.

He poked his head out and beckoned for Nada to follow him. She pushed past the branches, some of them pinging out and slapping Kane's face, then they stood together in front of a brick building, about the size of a one-car garage, a white UPVC front door to the far left. No windows, so he couldn't peek inside to see what the interior held.

He knocked on the door. Held his breath. Nada pushed out an exhalation beside him, and if her heart banged as fast as his, he sympathised with her. This was high-octane shit, and his sphincter clenched in anticipation.

Kane knocked again, harder this time.

Something hummed.

With no glass in the door or a letterbox to look through, he couldn't work out for the life of him what that noise was. A click, faint, then the door opened about an inch, a gold security chain preventing it going much farther.

A man in an orange boiler suit stared through the gap.

"Yeah?" he said. "Do you know what the bloody time is?"

"I'm well aware of the time, Mr Cobbings." Kane pulled out his warrant card, flashed it, then tucked it away. "DI Kane Barnett, and this is DS Nada Caridà. Can we have a word?"

"What about?" he asked, gruff as you like. "I'm busy, aren't I."

"What is this?" Kane gestured to the building.

"My man cave. Keeps me out of the missus' hair." The skin beneath his visible eye lifted, as did the corner of his mouth.

He was smiling, then.

You've got nothing to smile about, sunshine.

"I see," Kane said. "Well, so we don't disturb your *missus* by chatting out in the garden, or any of the neighbours come to that, we'd best come into your *cave* then, hadn't we."

Cobbings sighed. "If you insist."

The door shut, then the tinkle of the chain being removed sounded. Kane nudged Nada and nodded while staring at the door, so she'd get the gist they had to storm inside once it opened. Pulse thrumming, his chest fluttering with nerves, Kane waited.

The door opened, and Kane shot forward, forearms crossed in front of him, creating a battering ram, and he pushed at Cobbings, who staggered backwards, shouting "Fuck!" then righting himself. At the same time, Kane and Nada barrelled into him, sending him lurching in reverse, arms windmilling, one foot leaving the floor to point towards them. Cobbings went down, and Nada leapt on him, shoving him onto his front, jabbing her knee in his back and yanking his arms behind him, cuffing his wrists before Kane had a chance to help. She sat on the man then, ignoring him trying to buck her off, his legs going up and down, him working to kick her.

"Sir…"

Kane looked at her, then at where her attention was.

A body on a metal table.

What?

A woman on the floor.

A pool of blood beneath her head.

Long dark hair draped over her face.

God Almighty…

Kane rushed over there, Nada barking into her radio for assistance and an ambulance. He checked the woman on the floor first, moving some hair to press two fingers to her neck. A pulse, thankfully strong and steady.

"She's all right," he said, getting up to move to the side of the table.

This one wasn't.

The only way he could tell it was female was from the bra and the absence of a set of tackle between the legs. Everything else about her was just indicative of being human—a burnt human. Then bile raced up from his stomach at the sight of five fingertips—or was that a thumb there?— between the body's legs, and a…a…a bracelet on the wrist. A cheap plastic one, four blue dolphins dangling off it.

Oh God…

The sex worker's dolphin…

TWENTY-NINE

"This mess is connected to the sex worker." Kane's voice.

What?

Confused, the pain in her head threatening to murder her, Charlotte frowned, keeping her eyes shut. She didn't trust her ears—it must have been Henry who'd spoken. Yes, it was him, messing with her mind. How the hell had she not realised he had another side to him?

Because he never showed it to you, that's why.

There was that. He'd always been nice, but for him to have kept Jez's drugs for him all these years, done his dirty work? Jesus, she never would have imagined that.

"What do you mean, sir?" a woman asked.

Charlotte pressed her lips together and held back a shiver. Dare she hope she'd been saved? It was highly unlikely, what with the luck she'd had all her adult life. Good things didn't happen to her. This 'mess' just proved it. The stench of shit just got more gag-worthy the longer time wore on. And speaking of good, she'd always been that. Maybe it was time for her to go bad.

"What do you mean, sir?" someone mimicked. Another woman?

Charlotte cracked her eyes open, just enough so she could sip, not gulp, the view in front of her — she didn't think she could handle too much at once. Not after everything else she'd seen lately.

All that greeted her was her hair over her face. She slowly lifted her hand and parted the strands, praying Henry didn't notice, that he wasn't looking at her. Feet in black brogues, topped by black trousers, faint pinstripe. She'd love to say the person had put on burgundy socks with moss-green diamonds up the sides, but that would mean Kane *was* here, wouldn't it.

She shifted her attention to the right, and some woman sat on Henry's back — and it had to be Henry; that orange boiler suit like Jez's work one gave it away, except Jez didn't really need to use it because he didn't work in a fucking garage.

"The, uh, the victim — Christ — that poor woman on that table there has a bracelet on with the same dolphins as the one I spotted at the warehouse crime scene."

It was Kane, *it was.*

"It's not a woman," Charlotte said, her voice hoarse, and she pushed herself to sit up.

"*Charlotte?*" Kane shot down in front of her. "Bloody hell, I didn't realise it was you. How the hell did you *get* here?"

"Jez came for me." All her anxieties about this not really happening floated away, but then she looked at Henry, who stared at her from beneath that woman's arse, and anger raged, hot and sharp and wicked inside her. She pointed at him, then across the room. "Then *he* put him in there."

Kane glanced over his shoulder at the wardrobe. "Nada…"

So *that* was her name. The woman peered across the room. "Oh…"

Kane walked to where Jez's hand rested on the floor and bent to take his pulse. "He's gone."

Joy plunged into Charlotte, starting in her toes, swimming the crawl, eating up the distance until it reached her heart, then her head, where she blinked, disbelieving. It was obscene to feel this happy about someone dying, but... No, she wouldn't think about it now. She'd revel in it later, when she was alone.

Yes, she'd gone bad.

Kane returned to her, taking her hand and guiding her to stand. "What did you mean 'It's not a woman'?" He stared behind her.

"That's a girl," she said. "I...it's her shape, her size."

"A girl." Not a query, not echoing it as a question. "Shit." He faced Nada. "You *hear* that? Do you think it's...?"

She nodded.

"Fuck this fucking world, just fuck it." He slapped his forehead. "Get off *him*," he said, bright red spots tinging his cheeks, "and I'll take him back to the house. You stay here with the bodies, please, Nada."

"I'm coming with you," Charlotte said, grabbing his wrist, squeezing, pressing her need into him. "I don't want to be here with...them." She shivered, and her stomach cramped. She clutched it, nauseated and so anxious to get the hell away that she had the urge to bolt. The fresh air coming through the open door—a door she hadn't even thought was there—seemed to call out to her.

"Right." Kane pursed his lips then helped Nada up.

They hauled Henry standing by gripping one of his arms each and spun him to face the exit. Henry stared at her, and with the mannequin looking over his shoulder, the whole visual gave her the damn creeps. But she glared back, standing her ground—no man was ever going to have her cowering again. She'd steer clear of them if she had to, and where she planned on going, the only males she'd see were minimal.

Kane led Henry to the door, and Nada held Charlotte's elbow, guiding her behind the two men. Outside, Charlotte squinted at trees directly ahead.

"Where did he *take* me?" she asked.

"You didn't know, love?" Nada asked.

"I...I was in his house, then woke up in there." She jerked her thumb backwards.

Kane thrust Henry through the branches, and Nada patted Charlotte's shoulder to remind her to follow. She did, leaving Nada behind pushing through two trees to come out on the other side. She was in Henry's bloody back garden. Now she knew why it was smaller than hers, why he'd planted the trees. The sick bastard had had a steel room down here all along.

She swallowed bile — bile created by rage.

"Got a key, have you?" Kane said.

"Of course I sodding have," Henry said, "but the back door is open."

He didn't sound the same, like he was someone else entirely — mean and evil and without remorse for all the things he'd done. He'd be remorseful soon, Charlotte would put a bet on it.

In the house, she took the lead, showing the way to the living room. Kane shoved Henry so he flopped onto the sofa, wincing, no doubt uncomfortable with his hands cuffed behind him like that.

Good.

"What changed you?" she asked Henry. "Why don't you tell the nice policeman here. Why don't you explain how you can be a lovely, kind person on one side and a bastard on the other?"

Kane stood beside her, in front of the door, blocking the exit.

Charlotte dared to sit beside Henry. What harm could he do now? He'd already wrecked her just as much as Jez had, lied through his teeth for sixteen years, all the while pretending to be her friend, when really he'd just wanted to get into her knickers. He sickened her, and she mourned the loss of a man she'd trusted with all of her secrets, but not this version of the man, not the man next to her now.

"He killed Mrs Smithson," she said, glancing across at Kane. "I just don't understand it. She did nothing to you, Henry, she—"

"She lit those fires, and it's H1," he said. "H1, all right?"

"What?" Kane frowned.

"None of your business," Henry said. "And you want to know what changed me? Tough, because I'm not telling you."

Belligerent shit.

"I can tell you what changed him, Kane," she said.

"*Kane*, is it?" Henry stared at her, mouth slack and wet, his moustache quivering. "Bit familiar, isn't it, Char?" He looked at Kane. "Been up her fanny, have you?"

"Enough," Kane said. He raised his eyebrows at Charlotte. "What changed him?"

"His sister," she said.

And waited.

Henry head butted her, forehead crunching her nose, and she cried out in pain and shock, smacking backwards onto the arm of the sofa, one of the matted tassels from the pink pillows stroking her cheek. He was on her, humping her, his face coming closer, his lips nearing hers. She screeched with temper and tried to shove him up and off, but he was strong—so bloody strong—and then he wasn't there anymore.

She sat to find him on the floor, tossed there by Kane. Her nose throbbed, and she tasted blood at the back of her throat. Hot liquid oozed from one nostril, and she cuffed it away.

Henry wiped spittle off his chin by rubbing it against his shoulder. "I would have killed you and all, you know. Would have loved it, too. Bitch."

He rose so fast his movement blurred, and barged the side of his arm into Kane, smashing it into his face. Kane staggered back, bashing into the far corner, blinking as though he couldn't believe what had happened. As he surged forward to take hold of Henry, she caught a glimpse of the madness in Henry's eyes. He'd played the long game, reeling her in, and now the shit had hit the fan he had nothing to hide—and his madness wasn't hiding, it was there, stark as anything.

He lunged towards her, and she skipped to the side, darting around him. He turned to face her, and she knew he'd go for her again. Knew he felt thwarted by her, that he hadn't won the prize he'd been playing for.

There was only one winner in this game—and it would be her.

She grabbed the town crier's bell from the mantel.

And rang that motherfucker.

Kane halted his advance.

Henry's face showed shock, confusion, terror, and she kept ringing, staring at him, right in his eyes — eyes that no longer showed his kindness and honesty — reading the emotions in them. But instead of crumbling as she'd thought he would, he roared and went down on his knees.

"You won't beat me," he said. "You won't fucking beat me with…that."

"Try me." She shook the bell some more.

"I…I…"

She thought she had him, thought he'd broken then, until…

"I killed your mum, Char." He grinned, eyes gleaming with malice, and threw his head back, laughter billowing out of him.

Charlotte almost joined him on the floor, down on her knees, her whole world breaking apart. But she stayed standing, guilt at her mum being vulnerable to something like this because of her, fuming that he'd gone there and…and…

He bowed his head, and Charlotte brought the bell down, cracking it onto the back of his skull. And she kept cracking it, blood spurting, Kane shouting, his voice sounding far away, police sirens even farther still, and she didn't stop until Henry keeled over onto his side, unmoving.

Yes, if he was dead, where she was going, there would be limited men.

Not like you saw many in prison, was it.

"He attacked you, all right?" Kane said. "You hit him in self-defence, *okay*?" He shook her. "Charlotte. *Charlotte*. Listen to me."

If he thought he'd been crooked by paying a mate to run blood tests, he was bent right over now. Like a fucking pretzel. What a pissing mess.

She nodded, and he took the bell from her and placed it on the coffee table.

He held her in his arms—covered in blood, she was—but that didn't matter to him. While she sobbed, he wondered if this piece of scum had been telling the truth about Mrs Rothers. If he was… Jesus, how did a person get over that? How could Charlotte move on after this?

"Don't mention what he said about your mum," he warned her. "He nutted you, got on top of you, tried to take your clothes off with his teeth—"

"But he di-di-didn't, he—"

"Tried to take your clothes off, yes, and I came to pull him off you, and he threw me over there. I banged my head, couldn't get up for a minute or two, bit dazed, and by the time you'd hit him with the bell, it was too late for me to do anything, he was out cold. Got it?"

She nodded against his chest.

"You lost it, absolutely lost it, frightened because of what he'd done to you earlier, understand?"

"Yes."

He led her from the room, out into the hallway, and opened the front door. A police car swerved in front of an ambulance, and coppers and paramedics poured out. He gave directions to the room in the back garden, and a second ambulance arrived, the medics entering the house to see to Henry.

The bastard was still alive.

Kane stood in the Vine's living room, Ursula's wail tearing into his eardrums. Into his heart, if he were honest. The words he'd spoken —*We have reason to believe the body found this evening is that of Debbie*—were always the worst kind he ever uttered.

He didn't know what to do, not when Xavier sagged down onto the sofa, as though all the fight had been sucked out of him, holding his head in his hands and sobbing.

A man crying tugged at the emotions more than a woman somehow.

Nada glanced over at Kane from the door, her face showing she was an empath and not dealing with this too well. Maybe he ought not to have her as his partner, but perhaps she'd harden up, given time. Kane had thought *he* would get tough, back in his early days of being a copper, but look at him now, bottom lip trembling, his soul ripped to shreds from witnessing two people's lives being filleted in front of him.

A family liaison officer sat beside Ursula, and the couple would be in good hands with Julia. She'd get them through the first few days—then, unfortunately, they were on their own.

Kane cleared his throat. "I'm so sorry for your loss."

What else could he say?

And he left the room, Nada by his side, walking out of the house and into a future he wasn't sure he wanted to look forward to anymore.

This job... It had the ability to do you in.

EPILOGUE

Charlotte held her mum's hand and circled her fingertip over the diamond engagement ring. She imagined her dad working hard to pay for it, presenting it to his intended on bended knee, like her mum had told her he had.

Will I ever have that?

She had no idea, but to be honest, she'd gone off men for some reason.

"He went down for twenty-five to life, then," Mum said, staring at the news site on the laptop sitting on the kitchen table.

"Hmm."

The woman Charlotte once was didn't exist anymore. She didn't have dreams — not the right kind anyway — didn't think life would give her roses now she'd had her fair share of poison ivy. Didn't think she'd ever truly be happy until —

She was off to Cornwall. Starting a new life down there, on the tip of the land on which she'd endured so much. She hadn't expected to feel like this at thirty-something, tainted and bitter, everything decent in her soured.

Rotten.

Damaged.

But that's what happened when you got shit on, wasn't it?

It made you a bit twisted.

She sighed to hide a laugh.

"Reckon you'll tell that copper where you're going?" Mum asked.

"No. He's...he's not for me," Charlotte said. "Right, I'd best be off. Train's leaving in a few."

She hugged Mum, promised to keep in touch, but she wouldn't, it was better that way. Charlotte had things to do, and she couldn't do them if her mum was there as a constant, gentle reminder that you didn't have to let what happened to you define you.

Too late for that.

On the train, she used her new shiny laptop to compose a letter. The person she was writing to lived in Devon, not far from where she'd be renting a one-bed house. Close enough she could go visiting when the time was right.

She paused at the end of a sentence and stared at the countryside zipping by, the slight sheen of her reflection on the window. She was a blonde now, and she'd bought herself some specs — the kind you get for one ninety-nine in the cheap shops. She didn't look the same at all, and that was fine because she didn't feel the same either.

She finished the letter, and she'd print it out and send it once she arrived in Cornwall. This person she'd be pen pals with would be glad of her letters, she was sure. She'd help them feel better about themselves, give them sympathy, make them think she cared, and hopefully they'd ask her to meet them on one of those visiting passes. She'd build them up, lie to them for years if she had to, and then somehow, she'd finish what she'd started.

There was so much she had to accomplish, and sending her letter to the man serving twenty-five to life in HM Prison Dartmoor was just the beginning of a brighter future.

He didn't deserve to live, and she would make sure he didn't.

Good girl gone bad.

Printed in Great Britain
by Amazon

19335206R00161